THE WAR TRAIL

Four men were near death in that sun-bleached terrain and they no longer feared the Indians from whom they had escaped. Thirst was their enemy now and only two would live to see another day. Then into the picture came a husky young man called Dave Oak who was drawn to aid a girl grieving for her dead father and his missing inheritance. But what was the connection between the girl's father and the fleeing men? And what would make the Shoshones finally bury the hatchet?

DREW MARA

THE
WAR TRAIL

Complete and Unabridged

LINFORD
Leicester

First hardcover edition published in Great Britain
in 2003 by Robert Hale Limited, London

Originally published as *The War Trail*
by Mike M'Cracken

First Linford Edition
published 2004
by arrangement with
Robert Hale Limited, London

British Library CIP Data

Mara, Drew
 The war trail.—Large print ed.—
 Linford western library
 1. Western stories
 2. Large type books
 I. Title II. M'Cracken, Mike
 823.9'14 [F]

 ISBN 1–84395–412–5

Published by
F. A. Thorpe (Publishing)
Anstey, Leicestershire

Set by Words & Graphics Ltd.
Anstey, Leicestershire
Printed and bound in Great Britain by
T. J. International Ltd., Padstow, Cornwall

This book is printed on acid-free paper

JM

The Blue Giant

They were dying. They lay gasping in that arid, airless arroyo, and their desperate eyes looked hopelessly over the sun-bleached terrain ahead of them.

Now they no longer feared the Indian from whom they had been escaping. Now there was a more formidable enemy facing them with awful death.

One of the men, grey around the chin with unshaven stubble of more than a week, tried to lick his lips, but only a harsh rasping sound came from them. His voice croaked. 'We got to find water. We won't live more'n a few hours if we don't.'

One of his companions, lean, hardbitten, with all the makings of a range horseman gulped and then said painfully: 'There's one of us won't live those few hours anyway.'

He didn't lower his voice. He knew it wasn't necessary. The subject of his prophecy lay sprawled on his back, his bearded chin sagging open, with the breath of the man's life wheezing out of that open, pain-contorted mouth.

The first man who had spoken put out his hand to touch that recumbent figure. His voice was kind when he spoke. He said, 'I guess you're right. But we ain't leavin' him, all the same. There's always a chance for him if we meet up with water.'

And then the fourth member of their party drew attention to himself with a comment. He was a slouching, heavily-built fellow, with a face ravaged with deep lines that denoted a man of passionate temperament. His eyes were vicious now as he looked first at that recumbent man, and then at this desert-like valley in which they rested while the heat of the noonday sun beat fiercely upon them.

He growled: 'We ought to be thinkin'

of ourselves. We ought to be makin' tracks as fast as we can for the Platte. We didn't ought to be burdenin' ourselves with Ben.'

His brooding, savage eyes flickered from the lean horseman to the grey-stubbled veteran.

'He's a gonner,' the heavy man continued harshly. 'It don't help him to be lugged across country like we're doin'. I reckon it'd be a mercy if we left him here to die quietly in his sleep.'

There was no pause after his speech. That lean hard-bitten horse-man whirled on him like a savage, striking snake. 'Doggone, you, Tuff Leech,' he exploded. 'You c'n sit there an' talk like that after — '

That lean brown hand clenched around the stock of his Henry rifle. For a second while the temper blazed in him it almost seemed as though he would use that gun upon his compan-ion.

Tuff Leech came up at once with his own gun, and the two men sat and glared at each other with their fingers on the triggers and their guns pointing unwaveringly at each other's hearts.

Tuff Leech spat out words as if they were unclean. 'Don't you think you're gonner pull a gun on me, Lanky! I ain't to be shoved around by no no-good son of an Arizona cattle-thief!'

He was in a ferocious temper. His thirst was an agony, and he wanted to lash out and hurt, and he didn't care whom he hurt.

The older man intervened. He raised himself on his elbow, rubbed the dust out of his eyes and peered at his two companions, and then said, tiredly: 'Where does all this get you? You want to keep all the strength you've got, because by Glory you're gonner need it in the next hour!'

There was no sign of life. Only a few hours before that would have been gratifying. For they had been running from Indians for days now over the wild Laramie Range, and all the time they had been dreading the sight of fierce

4

warriors ranging after them on their nimble-footed ponies.

Their own horses were gone, shot from under them in the first ambuscade. They had got away because of the superiority of their weapons, and they had fought until nightfall in a running battle across the foothills. In the night they had slipped away from the Indian territory, only to face this other, terrifying enemy.

Thirst!

The old man spoke: 'While you two guys have been squabblin',' his voice rasped, 'I've bin thinkin'.' His eyes lifted to look with something like tenderness towards that lean cowboy who had strayed so far from the vast cattlelands of the south. He said: 'I figger, Lanky, you've got more strength in that skinny frame o' yourn than either of us.'

He got on to his knees, holding his precious rifle between his two work-worn hands. Now when he spoke his voice had something like an order in it.

'You, Lanky, will go on ahead and try and find water. We'll rest here and begin to follow when we can.'

That could mean, either when their companion had died and so relieved them of a burden, or when the sun was down sufficiently to permit of a coolness that would make travel more bearable than this awful heat.

Tuff Leech snarled. 'Why don't I go with Lanky? Ef you're so fond of Ben that you won't leave him, why'n Hades don't you just stay with him an' let us go on together?'

The old man's eyes met the speaker's sardonically. Drily he said: 'Mebbe there's a reason why you should stay behind an' help old Ben.' There was significance in his voice, and it wasn't lost upon his companions.

Lanky dragged himself to his feet. He swayed, his lean, tough body drained of strength as the result of their nightmare flight from the raging Indians, and these last hours in the desert without water.

He said: 'I figger you're right, Ezra. I'll go. I reckon there's no fear of Injuns now. I'll get water or bust. If I find water, I'll come back on my tracks to you.'

Ezra said. 'We'll be makin' all speed to come after you, Lanky, but I don't reckon we should move yet awhile.'

Lanky merely nodded as he began to lurch away on fatigue-stiffened legs towards the eastern opening to that wide, grassless arroyo. That was all the parting that Westerners expected. They might never meet again — probably wouldn't — but these tough frontier fighters hadn't time for sentiment.

He trudged on, head down, as if the sun's rays had physical weight and they were forcing him to the ground. Yet even though he walked as if the spirit had gone out of him, his hand never relaxed its grip upon his best friend — his rifle.

Two hours later he came out of that arroyo and found himself on the edge of vegetation. At first there were coarse bushes to break the arid monotony of this near-desert, and then small trees began to appear on the plain, finally merging into a narrow belt of tall, dark-leaved trees that clearly followed the windings of some stream or river.

That lean, hard-bitten ex-range-rider from Arizona was staggering as he entered the green belt. Here the grasses grew tall, almost to his shoulders, and there were times when his feeble arms could scarcely find the strength to part them.

Now, almost within sight of his goal, he was falling often, and where the ground sloped he had to crawl on hands and knees.

Behind him the grasses stirred.

Then, all at once he saw the fierce bright sunshine reflecting upon the surface of a broad stream. He heard the bright, sparkling waters as they rippled over the rough, rocky bottom of this mountain tributary of the mighty River Platte.

He went those last fifty yards at a

stumbling run. The movement in the bushes to his left quickened as he went.

He came down upon his knees in the mud on the edge of the stream, and his arms plunged to the shoulders in the cool, laving water. His head went under and he drank until he felt that he would burst. He drank until he had to come up for air because the water was over his face and in his eyes and up his nostrils while being gulped down that parched throat of his.

Panting, he pulled himself back away from the water, and then rolled on one side, heavenly relief flooding over him with the strength-giving water back in his body.

He saw something crouching within half a dozen yards of him. There was fear suddenly leaping into that Arizona puncher's eyes — but more than fear, even in that second before death struck him.

Then It was upon him. Before his hand had time to reach out and retrieve his rifle, death struck him in a savage flurry of quick blows.

Lanky lay still within a yard of the water that had given him new life and new hope. As he lay there, his face resting in the cool, comforting mud of the river bank something glittered near to his throat in the sunshine.

A hairy hand reached forward tentatively. It curled around that silvery object. A string looped through it and around the dead man's neck. A quick tug and it came away.

Then there was movement among those bushes again, and It retreated. They were waiting for Lanky back along the trail. Tuff Leach was wanting to go on and leave Ben, but that grey-chinned veteran of the plains had answered shortly, 'No.' And his rifle had been there to add compulsion to his wishes.

'We don't go while there's life left in old Ben,' Ezra, the older man, said shortly. 'An' we can't try to move him now. He's goin' out fast.'

The two men sat there while the sun

moved steadily round and began its descent towards the Laramie Mountains. It was torture, sitting there with the hot waves eddying from the sun-bleached rocks of that desolate arroyo.

The dying man held tenaciously on to life. They didn't know it, but in staying alive he was to save them — in standing by him it was, even for a short while, to save their own lives.

Miraculously, in some unaccountable way, both men fell asleep. It was the sleep of utter exhaustion.

It was then that that silent thing came walking openly up the trail towards them, hate in its heart.

They were helpless. They were asleep and at the mercy of the oncomer.

That mighty, nearly-naked figure looked down upon them, and those hairy hands clasped weapons that were red with the blood of the lanky puncher from Arizona.

But then one pair of eyes opened. It was Ben, perhaps opening his eyes for a last glimpse of the world that was slipping away from him. He was near to death, and yet suddenly for a few seconds his brain was clear and what he saw registered upon it.

Old Ben tried to call out to give warning, but no sound came from his throat. The sleepers slept on. That figure came nearer.

Then Ben found strength and his right hand began to move ever so slowly to where Tuff Leech's gun lay beside him. Those almost strengthless fingers fumbled about the trigger guard. There was insufficient life in his frame for him to lift that gun, but even as his life again began to recede from him, he yet found strength to pull upon the trigger.

The sound of that gun exploding was deafening. It brought Leech and his older companion upon their elbows in an instant. They peered in horror through the swirling white smoke from that Henry rifle.

They were in time to see that weird figure sway and then slowly crumple.

They saw a blue man — a man painted vivid blue from his hair down to his toes. He wore a mask upon his face — a carved wooden mask that was full of evil things, like snakes that bit poison-ously and scorpions and other crawling things that were of no use to man. That was what was carved on that hideous wooden mask.

And around his waist was a girdle of bones, and all the bones were human. But they saw that mighty, seven-foot blue figure toppling like a felled pine, with tomahawk and scalping knife dropping from hands suddenly nerve-less.

The older man got to his feet, and stood swaying there, peering like a man in a daze around him. Then in an awed voice, he said: 'Ben did it. It was the last thing he did, but by Glory he saved our lives!'

His eyes flickered sardonically towards Tuff Leech at that. His rasping voice said: 'Aye, Tuff, he saved your life an' with your rifle, too.' Then they walked across to where that blue figure lay in the dust. Ezra turned him over. He saw that covered face and it never occurred to him to pull off the mask and see what lay beneath it. They were too exhausted even for the little effort of stooping and tearing away the hideous carved wooden mask upon that blue giant sprawling in the dust.

All they could think, looking down, was: 'We had a lucky escape. This feller would have done for us while we slept but for poor old Ben.' Only Tuff Leech didn't think of their departed companion as 'Poor old Ben.'

Leech said harshly, 'He's dead. That was a break for us.'

Then his dark, glittering eyes shifted to Ben and he said, 'He's dead, too.' Back came his eyes to meet his companion's. 'Now there ain't no reason why we should stay in this hole. I don't figger there's much life left in me, but I aim to keep movin' and get out of this valley an' try an' find water before I cash in my chips.'

Ezra nodded. His voice was harsh as he looked eastwards across the desert waste. 'We'll go now,' was all he said.

They left a man for dead, but less than half an hour after they had moved that big, blue giant slowly stirred and sat up. The bullet which had ricochetted from a rock and struck upwards under his mask had given him only a glancing blow — sufficient to lay him unconscious and yet scarcely wounding him by more than a scratch.

The blue giant clambered to his feet, the strength returning into those mighty limbs. He went across to the dead man, but didn't touch him. Then he sought around until he found the trail of the pair who had got away.

2

The Champion

Scalping Knife, that frontier town on the River Platte, was crawling with excitement. Men riding in felt it in the air.

When the newcomers rode into the town that was chock full of men, they were told, 'Don't you know? Today's the big fight. Jacques Lecleux, the Ontario champ, is here to meet the Missouri Mauler. Brother, you're in time to see a danged good fight!'

Sitting back from the throng, on some steps of a skin-packing establishment right at the end of the main street, a big young man watched it all and failed to get enthusiastic about the fight.

He was sitting in the shade, a floppy-brimmed hat stuck at the back of his head, showing black curly hair that was matted with sweat. His face was big — almost it could be described as massive. There was a lot of solid bone and muscle about that face, and yet it wasn't a hard face, as so many men's were in this mountain country. There was even a feeling of mildness behind the good-humoured expression in his blue eyes.

He was dressed much like any other man on the Western trails of that day. He wore a shirt that had been bleached into a nondescript shade of red by the suns of many American states. His pants were of homespun cloth and were tucked into the inevitable riding boots. Only, this man had no horse. He was thinking about that as he sat there and let the dry sand of the main street filter between his long, capable fingers.

So it was that this lone spectator, unheeding the general excitement as the time of the big fight drew near — he alone saw that small, trail-dusty figure stagger into the town.

At first he thought the man was drunk. There were plenty drunk around the town right then. Then his sharp eye detected something different in the manner in which this bowed and tottering figure came so painfully to the first of the buildings along the main street.

The big young husky saw that old, stubble-chinned man collapse out of exhaustion against the wall of the first clapboard building.

He got up then and hitched his pants and went striding quickly across. Someone inside that first building must have heard the thud of the body falling against the warped boarding. As the big young fellow came tramping up the door opened and someone looked out. There was a muttered conversation, and then quickly three men appeared and came down and stood over that recumbent figure.

The young husky found himself staring down upon the trail-worn newcomer over the bending heads of

18

three unprepossessing young men — three men who by the smell of it had been drinking together within that first building.

The young husky heard the rambling voice of a man in delirium. 'Got to find . . . ' the man kept saying. He'd get so far, 'Got to find . . . ' but never seemed to be able to say what he'd got to find.

And then a few more words trickled out. 'It was a blue Injun, I tell you. Blue . . . blue as the hills of Virginny. He did for Lanky, I reckon . . . '

The words went on, bubbling in delirium from the lips of this man who was out of his mind.

The young husky heard one of the three spectators mutter sullenly, quickly, 'It's Ezra Hallet!' And the way he said it suggested that Ezra Hallet was a person of importance.

Then the three must have felt the shadow of the big young husky upon them, because their heads came wheeling round so that he looked into suddenly startled, suspicious eyes.

The young giant didn't miss a thing. Then he said, his voice drawling and casual-sounding, 'You know him?'

The three men looked at each other, and there was a veiled warning in the glances that interchanged. One of them nodded. 'Sure we know him. He's a — a kinda friend of ours.'

The young newcomer looked down at that moaning, raving man. 'I figger he's wounded,' he said, his eyes noting the dark stain on the man's thigh, showing even against the dark material of the old man's pants. 'An' by the sound of it he's out of water. Mebbe one of you had better get a drink for him.'

He moved forward, as if about to take charge of the delirious man. It was the action of a man purposeful and ready to take command of a situation.

But he was halted by a quick grasp on his arm. It was Jeff, the quick-witted spokesman for the trio. The husky looked into eyes that flashed a warning, for all that the words spoken were conciliatory enough. 'You don't have to worry, stranger. I tell you, Ezra's a friend of ours. We'll see to him.'

The husky halted. He couldn't push himself in when men spoke of friendship, and yet he felt uneasy. He stood by and watched them as they picked up that old man and carried him up the short flight of steps to the raised boardwalk that fronted the buildings on this main street.

The last thing he heard was, 'I know where it is. Enough for a lot of men, I reckon . . . I got to find . . . '

He was on the old subject again. He'd got to find someone but he never said who or what.

The husky turned away. He was remembering that last glimpse of the old man. Remembering how, as they'd carried him feet first up those few steep steps that led on to the raised boardwalk, something had slipped from under the shirt of the old man. It was something silver, slung on a cord around the stricken man's neck.

It was behind the saloon that the big fight between the Canadian, Jacques Lecleux, and the Missouri Mauler was to be held. The big young husky knew quite a lot about that fight by now — how a purse for a thousand silver dollars had been put up by a group of mine owners, flushed with wealth and avid for some entertainment, here in the backwoods of the State.

But he knew something else, too, and it made him faintly uneasy to contemplate it. There wasn't going to be a big fight that night!

He ambled down that deserted, dusty main street, and his thoughts alternated between the stricken man back there in that hut with those three uninspiring 'friends', and the loss of his horse earlier that day. The thought of his loss made him suck the knuckles of a right hand that was still very sore. In the distance he saw the flutter of a gaily-coloured dress. He halted in his tracks, his eyes widening.

'A gal!' he muttered to himself. This was no place for girls, he thought disapprovingly. This was a rough town, in a man's country. It wasn't good for a girl to be walking the streets alone.

Then he had another surprise. The girl was walking determinedly across towards the alley that gave behind the Wildcat saloon.

'Goldarn it, ef she ain't a'goin' to that there fight herself,' he exclaimed in surprise. Again he shook his head. Fights were all right for men, but women should never attend them.

He had no intention of going near that noisy throng. And he had good reason for keeping away. In fact, if he had had a horse he wouldn't have been in this town now at all —

Two grim, silent men stepped out from a doorway and barred his path. He saw eyes that were narrowed against the long slanting rays of the setting sun, and they were hard and without mercy. Then his eyes dropped to the thighs of those two silent men. He saw four hands, and each grasped the butt of a worn and workmanlike Colt.

He knew those men. They knew him, too, which was a whole lot worse. He kept his hands spread apart, to show daylight between them and his own guns. He wasn't going to trade lead with these *hombres*, not with them having such a start on him where gunplay was concerned.

He licked his lips and waited. He didn't say anything because there wasn't anything he could say. He just stood there on the board sidewalk, his big shoulders hunched, and that massive, heavily-boned face impassive as he regarded them. One of the *hombres* jerked his head, indicating the alleyway across the road from them. At that moment there was a savage yell from the unseen crowd behind the saloon. There was the anger in that tone that spoke of men cheated of something they prized highly.

The big young husky knew what it was.

There was no alternative. He swung round on the heel of his boot made for riding and not for walking.

When they were marching between the high wooden walls of that alley, yet another savage roar went up from the crowd beyond. This time the roar continued.

Again that big husky licked his lips, and this time he did turn, his eyes looking swiftly and rather desperately under the brim of his hat at those two silent gunmen behind him.

At that they broke their silence. One lean, brown face cracked open and permitted the passage of a few diamond-hard words. 'Scared, huh? I figger you ought to be scared! Wait till that crowd get to know who you are, brother!'

He turned the corner. There was confusion everywhere — confusion and unceasing noise.

He saw a natural basin immediately below the Wildcat Saloon. He couldn't see the ring because of the crowded people all standing and shouting before him, but he knew it was at the bottom of the little basin. Grouped solidly around this natural amphitheatre were probably the better part of a thousand men, and every man was red, roaring angry. The noise was tremendous.

Those two gunmen closed up behind the husky then, and he felt himself being prodded forward on the point of that gun barrel. His eyes flickered over the red angry faces, over the bobbing hats of the excited spectators. He saw that girl standing aloof from the crowd, and it seemed to him there was pleasure on her face alone. He couldn't see what she had to be pleased about.

But in that quick glimpse he saw a face that struck into his mind so that ever afterwards when he closed his eyes he could see it. He saw a fine face, a head that was erect and proud. It was the face of a true frontiersman, handsome and unafraid, with spirit in every flash of her bright blue eyes. The wind was stirring now and her hair fluttered within the protection of a blue band of ribbon that sought to gather the luxuriant tresses together.

His captors forced him right to the ropes, where forms and rough seats had been set up for the more distinguished patrons — for those wealthy mine-owners who had put up the purse-money for this attractive fight. Then they ordered him to halt, so that he faced a ring that was nearly as crowded as the sloping hillside around it.

Inside it was a man who clearly was one of the contestants. He was massive, with the broken nose and battered ears of his calling. He was standing with a towel round his bare, hairy shoulders, clad only in a pair of fancy jeans. His feet were naked.

The others in the ring were just people, so far as the young husky was concerned. A lot of men all arguing and shouting at each other. Then, a few minutes later, someone roared for silence. He got it in time. It was the proprietor of the Wildcat saloon himself.

He hollered: 'Ef you don't shut your danged mouths a minute there won't be no drinkin' in the Wildcat tonight. Goldarn it, don't you know I'm jest as disappointed as you are!'

Then he shouted again. 'But there ain't nothin' I can do about it. They tell me the Missouri Mauler's been hurt in an accident an' he can't come to Scalpin' Knife for the fight today.'

At that there was a roar of rage from the crowd and the husky could hear men furiously shoutin. 'They're hedgin' on bets! They've got cold feet and are backin' out! They know Lecleux's got the beatin' of the Mauler!'

Again the bull-necked, grizzle-headed saloon-keeper roared for silence. 'It's the truth that I'm telling you. The Mauler met with an accident. I've just been told how he came by that accident.'

Something in the way the saloon-keeper spoke gripped the attention of that throng and this time they became completely silent, wanting to know what the saloon-keeper had to tell them.

'The Mauler got himself chopped down by a feller who jumped him when his back was turned!'

The husky's head lifted at that, his eyes lost their uneasiness and instead went steely hard. His big fists clenched at his side.

The saloon-keeper went on, his eyes now never leaving that husky. 'There are men here who saw it happen. There was some bother over a horse, and then the fellar jumped the Mauler and hit him so hard when he wasn't looking that he put him out and he won't be any good for days now, they tell me.'

A swelling roar went up from that angry mob.

The saloon-keeper couldn't be heard this time above the din of threatening voices. But every man there was able to see, and they saw the hairy forearm of that muscular saloon-keeper extend and point towards a big husky standing between two silent, grim-faced trail riders. And they saw that one of the trail riders had a gun and it was pressed hard into the back of that young cowboy.

In that second the big young husky acted characteristically. He gave a shove, and the trail rider on his left went sprawling into the crowd. He risked a bullet in his back with that movement, but he took a chance.

He walked forward and ducked between the ropes and went up to that saloon-keeper, who stood eyeing him grimly. Back of the saloon-keeper reared the battered faces of the Ontario champion and his supporters. Every eye was riveted upon the big, broad-shouldered husky.

Quite clearly his voice rang out, though even now it sounded leisurely, with a southern drawl in it.

'I don't know who told you that story, barman, but it ain't correct.' The big husky turned and looked at that crowd that faced him on all sides. He lifted his voice. 'I never hit any man unawares. He asked for trouble and I sure gave it him.'

Standing there in the middle of that hostile crowd his thoughts went back to his adventure earlier that day. It was on the trail coming westward towards the Laramie Mountains and the California side of the Rockies. He had been sleeping, content to let his mount carry him along the dusty, uneventful trail.

He hadn't expected trouble on the trail going in to Scalping Knife, because this side of the country was well settled and free from warring Indians.

He must have been overtaken by a party of hard-galloping horsemen, one of whom thought to play a trick on the sleeping Westerner.

The young husky had found himself rudely awakened when his screaming horse went down between his legs. Instinctively he had kicked free of his spurs and gone rolling into the mesquite, leaping to his feet almost the instant he touched earth.

He'd swayed to his feet, conscious of his horse, still kicking and screaming in high-pitched tones of pain, while before him, rope in hand, was a big, ugly, battered-faced individual in smart clothes clearly obtained from New York or Washington or at least some place far east of the Laramie Range.

Alongside the big, battered individual were other horsemen, all grinning in wicked humour at sight of the husky's abrupt awakening.

The husky had seen something that the others hadn't noticed. In that fall his horse had broken a leg. He saw the unnatural way it was bent, and he knew that that trick had ruined a good horse and he would have to part with an old comrade.

His first thought was to use his guns, but then, even before his hands made the move to those twin butts clasped against his thighs, he stayed them. Instead he took two giant strides forward and that carried him against the big Easterner grinning down at him from the saddle.

The husky reached up and tore the rope out of the other's hands — that rope that was still wrapped around the kicking legs of his mount. Then the Texan's big hand gripped the shirt neck of the heavy rider and jerked him right out of his saddle.

The others should have found warning in that action. It took a man of incredible strength to reach so high and in such easy manner tear a big man loose from his saddle and throw him to the ground. But they hadn't much sense, anyone in that party.

Even less sense was in that battered face of the infuriated rider with the cropped ears, swaying to his feet in the dust.

He was brushing his clothes, his little eyes under those puffed eyebrows glaring hatred at the young husky facing him. He was snarling savage oaths, saying what he would do.

It was then that the husky heard the

name of the Missouri Mauler for the first time. He was not afraid.

He was in a blind, savage rage himself. It was a doggoned, low-down trick, to get a man off his horse like that. It might have broken his neck by the unexpectedness of his fall. As it was, it had broken his horse's leg, and in a moment he would have to shoot it out of hand.

The Mauler didn't expect attack, but it came. It came so swiftly that the other men, the Mauler's friends, had no time to intervene.

The husky leapt in, and in a matter of seconds the fight was all over. The Mauler tried to crash a ponderous right that would have altered the features of that young husky considerably, but it never landed.

The husky swayed and the blow travelled over his shoulder. Then he was inside those mighty, muscular arms of the professional boxer. He was inside, and his own left fist was travelling in a wicked arc that connected with the square jaw of the fighter and jerked the man's head back on his thick-set neck.

Then the husky came slamming through with a right that was terrible to watch. It came with all the strength of that angry man behind it. It seemed to be travelling a long way, but then he was a big man with a long reach. That fist crashed not quite where it was intended. That blow to the chin had tilted the head of the professional boxer and it had exposed the muscular neck below the Mauler's left ear.

The Mauler went down in an agony he had never known before. That mighty blow had torn the muscles of his neck, and though the Mauler was not knocked out he was in such frantic pain that he had no thoughts of continuing the fight.

His supporters leapt from their horses and ran to the side of their fallen comrade. One of them, a stocky, oldish man, who also bore the marks of the ring upon his face, seemed to know what he was about. He examined the writing Mauler on the ground and then got to his feet, his face livid with passion. 'That's done for the Mauler!' he shouted savagely. 'Doggone it, he won't fight for weeks with a neck like that!'

That brought those men round, fury on their faces. Their hands were leaping for their guns.

They saw the young husky crouching there, twin guns already in his massive fists. The eyes that looked at them from above those twin blue muzzles were hard and unwavering.

'I wouldn't do anythin' rash with them guns o' yourn!' the young husky drawled. 'As sure as my name's Dave Oak, I'll let you have lead as soon as look at you!'

He was still raging. He jerked a barrel of his gun. 'Get that carcass on to a hoss an' get on your way!' he ordered icily. 'I've an unpleasant job to do!'

He meant his horse. It was in pain and he wanted to shoot it quickly to relieve it from further suffering. But he

36

couldn't do that — couldn't turn his back upon them — while they were there.

Sullenly they got the pain-wracked Mauler on to his horse and then the party rode westward towards Scalping Knife. When they were gone, the young husky, who had named himself Dave Oak, went to his horse.

It was a thing he hated to do. He loved this fine animal that had been his range companion these last five or six years.

And then, with heavy heart, he tramped the last few miles into Scalping Knife.

Evidently the Mauler had been taken to some outlying cabin, because neither he nor his party had been apparent in the town when big Dave Oak walked in. He was flat broke, and couldn't buy a horse, and so, whether he wanted to or not, he was forced to remain in this town that had been the objective of his newly-made enemies. He couldn't help that.

But now he was being called to account for what he had done.

He saw the savage eyes of a crowd cheated of its enjoyment all fixed evilly upon him. Just as furious was Lecleux, the Ontario champion. Dave heard angry comments from Lecleux's supporters, and gathered they had come all this way for nothing. No fight, no prize money. That made Lecleux and his friends mighty sore at this young husky. The saloon-keeper took it on himself to try the husky almost as if he were a judge.

'What in heck did you lay hands on the Mauler for?' he shouted roughly, speaking loudly so that the crowd could hear.

Oak faced him resolutely. 'He played a joke on me!' he retorted. 'A dirty trick. He roped my horse while I was sleepin' an' broke a foreleg!'

'But you didn't need to hit him from behind!'

'That's what them doggone critters told you!' Dave Oak said contemptuously, waving towards the pair of trail

38

riders who had brought him in. His eyes swept that crowd challengingly. 'But it didn't happen like that. I threw him off his hoss, and then I knocked him out!'

His voice was contemptuous.

'He wasn't much of a fighter. I kinda stroked him a coupla times an' he jes' curled up an' hollered for mamma!'

They all heard him, there on the surrounding hillside. At his words a savage shout went up from the crowd and they came surging forward as if intent upon tearing this big, husky stranger from limb to limb.

His wrist's were gripped by men of the Lecleux faction. He found himself a prisoner there in the ring with a mob intent on getting in at him and beating him up because he had spoilt their pleasure.

Curiously at that moment he was able to see that girl — that lovely young creature who had come down the alley before him. She was behind the crowd, watching over their heads from the rim of this natural arena.

Then a surging movement of that turbulent crowd and she was lost to view.

Dave Oak lashed out. Those men from the Canadian's camp tried to hold on to him, but either he was stronger than they had imagined or the unexpectedness of his resistance upset them.

Dave Oak whirled and faced those other men in the ring, including the massive, brutalized Lecleux himself, and the saloon-keeper, who made these matches for the benefit of his trade. His hands went again for his guns. They weren't there. Those men had lifted his guns even in the act of grasping him by the wrists.

He was unarmed and at the mercy of this raging mob.

A shout went up from the back of that swaying throng. 'Let Lecleux get at him!'

At once the crowd leapt at the idea.

'Turn Lecleux loose on him!' The cry rang around the ring.

All in one moment a match had been arranged. The saloon-keeper was shoving Oak back into a corner, his face grimly satisfied. 'You've got to fight, son. You asked for this, now get out of it any way you can!'

His tone was vicious. He had a reputation as a match-maker to keep up and this was the biggest fight he had arranged. He hated the drawling young husky at that moment, and all he asked was that Jacques Lecleux would cut him to ribbons.

Then his eyes saw the hairy chest that came out from under that faded shirt and his brows contracted. It was the kind of chest you see once in a lifetime. It was . . . mighty!

When he saw those biceps he turned and looked at Lecleux, stripping to his pants in the far corner, and there was an expression of doubt on his face, as if he wasn't so sure Lecleux would give this upstart' a good hiding.

Lecleux had no doubt. He was eager to demonstrate his prowess before this crowd, and the fact that it was an easy match only pleased him the more. His seconds were sneeringly confident and cocky. As they prepared their man for the ring they glanced over their shoulders and smiled bitingly at the big husky in the far corner.

There were no gloves. They had started using gloves back in New York, but as yet the fashion hadn't spread into the West. They were regarded as effeminate.

A roaring, cheering crowd, content to see butchery if they were deprived of their sport, sent up a loud cheer as the saloon-keeper called the contestants into the middle of the ring.

He told them that kicking was barred, that scratching wasn't a thing that should be done, and they'd to keep their thumbs out of each other's eyes. As he stepped back his eyes again looked at those bronzed muscles of the young giant, and he was more thoughtful than the vainglorious Lecleux.

His face was grim as he lifted his fists

to guard his face. He hadn't wanted this fight. He didn't believe in fighting. But by Glory, it had been forced upon him and he'd show this swaggering Canadian that a Texan knew how to use his fists as well as his guns!

Lecleux came in, his shorn head tucked down among the mighty muscles of shoulders that were big enough for an ox. His little eyes glittered over the top of his tightened fists. There was a little grin upon lips that had taken many a battering.

They took one now.

An astonished crowd saw the young husky leap in, with an incredible savagery in that forward motion. They saw a right hand stab out so swiftly they hadn't really time to see whether it was a hook or a jab. It hit Lecleux smack upon the mouth, and Lecleux collapsed through the ropes.

There was a moment of silence. Then that crowd let out a gasp and began to talk among themselves, and the murmur filled the evening air in a growing sound that became a roar of delight.

They got Lecleux and shoved him back into the ring. He was shaking his head. His seconds were telling him, 'You weren't lookin'. You should've got out of the way of that!'

The bruiser lost his temper and came back with his arms swinging. He ripped into big Dave Oak and brought big red weals to those mighty ribs. He slapped the husky upon the side of his head and then pinned a granite-like fist under the Texan's chin.

It hurt Dave. He stepped back and shook his head. Lecleux was after him, giving him no rest. His fists were pounding, battering at the ribs and then lifting to smack at Dave Oak's head. Then the barrage of blows came down upon that chest again and sought to find a weakness in the stomach . . . and then hit in cowardly fashion below the belt.

Dave grasped him by the ears. That was a legitimate hold in those days. He took Lecleux in a run across the ring, because Lecleux had to go where his ears went, and then Dave threw him with all his might over the topmost rope, into the lap of the wealthy patrons who had had seats brought out for them.

Dave stalked around that ring like a lion angered beyond control. He hadn't wanted this fight, he shouted at the saloon-keeper, his big chest heaving. By Glory, did he have to kill Lecleux to show that he wasn't wanting a fight?

It wasn't quite understandable. All the saloon-keeper knew was that this enraged young Texan had the beating of the champion of Canada.

An astonished crowd was coming round to the idea, too. They had never witnessed such mighty strength. Now they began to cheer the Texan.

He would have gone from the ring then, but they wouldn't let him. He had to stay there and knock out the Canadian before he could go. When he realized that he shrugged his shoulders and waited until Lecleux came clawing back through those ropes, hatred on his ugly face. Lecleux just couldn't believe he was receiving such rough treatment at the hands of an amateur.

Dave Oak leapt to meet him. This time he wasn't going to take any more punishment. If he had to lay out this Lecleux, then he was going to do it pronto!

Lecleux fought madly, but Dave Oak had the reach on him. That solid right fist of the young husky kept banging on to Lecleux's bent nose. In time he could hardly see because of the pain it gave him. And then Dave began to slog at a stomach exposed, and again, though Lecleux fought back, it didn't save him.

There came a moment when Lecleux was staggering, trying to protect his stomach and leaving his face exposed. Dave Oak swung and hit him, and he hit him so hard that it almost threw the Texan out of the ring himself. He didn't bother to look at Lecleux, fallen in his corner. Dave Oak knew when he hit a man like that he didn't rise within a few minutes.

He was grabbing his shirt, wanting to get away from this crowd that came surging forward now, every man his friend and wanting to treat him to a drink and pat him on his back and say what a fine fighter he was.

And then they heard a shout from the top of the hill.

A man was standing there. He was holding on to the back porch rail of the saloon, and there was excitement on his face and a note of urgency in his voice. Dave Oak paused, his shirt draped over one shoulder, his old hat perched on the back of his head. Someone was shoving guns back into his belt.

That voice rang down to them. 'There's been a massacre! Three whites have been killed and one's got through with only a little life left in him!'

The light wasn't too good, and Dave, peering, couldn't be certain, but he thought he had seen that speaker before. He wondered where, and then realized that it was one of the three men who had taken in the delirious old man who had talked about a blue Indian.

That voice came down to him again.

'They ambushed them. They were wiped out — massacred. All but one man who got through — and won't live!'

That crowd forgot all about Dave Oak and the fallen Lecleux at that. Massacre!

That was an ugly word to hear along that frontier. The reaction upon those men was instantaneous. The crowd began to surge and break up and go running towards their huts where their rifles and horses were. They didn't permit the massacre of their kind. If Indians rose against the white man, then the white man rode against the Indians to demand swift and terrible retribution.

Big Dave Oak, pulling on his shirt, climbed out of that basin that had been a stadium almost unobserved.

The town was a seething mass of men dashing into buildings and coming out and leaving the doors slamming. Horses were being saddled and bridled and dragged out into the street. Hundreds of men were going on this expedition, and it wasn't possible to walk down that main street for fear of being trampled on.

Dave avoided that main street and went walking round the backs of the buildings. He was thinking. There was something that didn't satisfy him. Mainly he was thinking of that shifty-eyed man who had shouted the news to the crowd at the end of the fight.

He was wondering why he had done it. Because a man like that only did things to his own advantage. He didn't look the kind of man to be much concerned about justice, not even where it affected the white man's interests in the West.

Dave knew men, just as he knew horses and cattle. And he was thinking that that man was a rogue and rogues ran to a pattern.

'He's up to something,' Dave told himself. 'He's makin' monkeys out of these fellars,' was his hunch.

So now instead of trying to find a horse and join the posse, he went walking round the backs of these buildings, intent upon finding that old man, by the shifty-eyed one's account, the sole survivor of a massacred party.

He didn't reach that hut immediately. Someone reached out from an alleyway that was shadowy because the sun was almost spent. He felt fingers grip on to his arm and that brought him wheeling round, his hands going instinctively for his guns.

3

The Quarter Dollar!

A sharp voice said: 'You don't need to pull a gun on me, mister.'

Dave relaxed at once. He turned and found himself looking at the girl — the girl he had seen watching the fight.

Close to, she was lovelier than he had imagined. She was fair, and her hair was pulled back and tied with a ribbon. She had blue eyes — eyes that were lovely, even though at the moment they looked at him frostily and with contempt. She looked attractive in a gaily-patterned dress of material clearly imported from the East.

But though she wore a dress of city origin, Dave saw that she was no Easterner, but a true frontierswoman. He was glad of it.

He heard that girl's voice ring out

coldly: 'Why do you have to fight?'

Dave could only look at her in surprise.

'You men should be ashamed of yourselves, going into a ring and pounding each other to a jelly just to provide amusement for a lot of stupid, drunken men!'

Dave was bewildered. His mouth opened to say something, but he just couldn't think of the appropriate words, and so it stayed open, sagging like a fish.

The girl spoke sharply, her eyes holding Dave's. 'Well, why don't you answer me? Or are you ashamed?'

Dave gulped. He shifted awkwardly on his high-heeled riding boots. He felt less sure of himself before this slip of a girl than he had with the formidable Lecleux. Then he found words, and they were a protest.

'I didn't want to fight, ma'am.' He shrugged those mighty shoulders. 'I was kinda forced into it,' he said good humouredly.

'Forced nothing!' The girl's voice was abrupt. 'You men always make excuses. But you know you wanted to fight, otherwise you wouldn't have been down there at the ring.'

She turned away at that as if having delivered her reproof she felt she had done all she could in the interests of peace. She began to walk away quickly.

Dave caught up with her in two huge strides.

He was confident now, able to match up with her.

'I figger you don't like fightin' men?'

A very cold, 'No, I don't!' came from her lips.

Dave found himself wanting to make that pretty face smile, wanted to see her eyes look upon him with friendliness and not in such hostile manner.

He said: 'I know how it is. Women jest don't take to men's rough games.' He sighed. 'Mebbe I don't altogether disagree with you, ma'am,' he said. And then he repeated, 'But I didn't want to go into that fight. I just had a gun in my back and couldn't get away.'

She turned on him then. 'Oh,' she said sarcastically, 'and why don't you like to fight other men? Why are you so different?'

The huge Texan by her side seemed to halt at that and lift his eyes to an horizon that was back in his past, as if he was looking over well-remembered events.

Then he sighed and said: 'Every time I get into a fight the other fellar gets hurt. That's the way it's always been. You don't get much fun out of knockin' a fellar down,' he went on apologetically. 'So I kinda keep out of fights because I don't want to go knockin' men flat on their backs and hurtin' them.'

It was the girl's turn to be startled. There was a genuine ring of truth about this giant's statement. For one second she thought it could be true, that this man really didn't like to get into fights because of the monotony of their ending.

And then she shook her head. She wasn't going to be taken in by such talk. She knew that all men were alike, just brutal children, who were never happier than when they were damaging each other. Well, she had made her protest, and now she wanted to get away from this big hulk of a man.

They were just crossing an alleyway that gave a view of the crowded street beyond. Men on horse-back were surging around, trying to pull themselves into an orderly column and not succeeding because their horses were restive and inclined to buck and rear and do everything but behave in orderly manner. Someone must have seen them. There was a shout from the shadows where the lighted windows of a saloon accentuated the evening's dusk.

They halted. A man came running towards them. He was an older man than most, and that was perhaps why he was not mounted with the others. He came stumbling up, his eyes upon the girl.

She said, sharply: 'What's the matter, Amos?'

That old man didn't speak until he was right up to her. Because of it Dave knew there was serious news for this girl to know. The girl must have sensed it, too, because he heard her quick drawn breath in anticipation of bad news. Again she said, 'What is it, Amos?'

That kindly old man came and took her hand in his. He said: 'You've got to be a brave little gal, Sue. I've got news for you you won't like.'

The girl's voice came quickly: 'Father?'

Amos nodded.

Sue seemed to stumble into his arms, suddenly frantic to know the worst. She was gripping that old man by his rough shirt front. 'Tell me, Amos, what has happened? Is he back?'

Amos nodded, his grey eyes looking compassionately at that frightened face before him. He patted her shoulder.

'He's back, Sue. An' I'm afraid — ' His voice trailed away.

There was a sob from the girl, interpreting the significance behind that unfinished sentence.

'He's badly hurt?'

'He's badly hurt.'

The girl pulled herself together. 'Take me to him,' she said. Amos put his arm across her shoulder as if to give her comfort in her moment of distress, and he led her behind those sprawling huts that made up a single main street. Dave stood where he was, forgotten in this moment of drama. He watched after the pair.

Suddenly his eyes narrowed, guessing their destination. His hunch was right. He saw them enter a hut by the rear door, and it was the farthermost hut of this little township — the hut into which that delirious old man had been carried by those three shifty-eyed, unprepossessing individuals.

He turned away. He went round to that saloon whose owner brought trade to the town by staging prize fights. It was a more friendly saloon-keeper who saw him now, in a saloon with few occupants because most of the town's people were riding out to effect retribution upon the Shoshone Indians, reputed to be the authors of the massacre.

Dave was blunt in his demands. He hadn't wanted to fight, but he'd been forced into it. Okay, he'd fought — and won. Now, what was the prize?

Even though he was in a good humour and friendly that saloon-keeper tried to keep a good bargain. He'd had his fight, and he hadn't been called on to pay out any prize money to date. He didn't intend to if he could. He said so.

So, to the delight of the few men remaining in that saloon, big Dave reached across the bar, took that rascally saloon-keeper by the throat and yanked him over the broad, well-worn counter. In that position, helpless, Dave told him, quietly, but very determinedly, what he would do to that no-good hossthief of a saloon-keeper if he didn't think up a prize right away.

The saloonkeeper didn't want to choke and said weakly: 'You tell me what you want. Just get your big paws off my throat. I don't like it.'

Dave said, evenly, without releasing his hold upon that unshaven throat, 'I want a hoss — a good one. I figger I earned it. Do I get one?'

The saloonkeeper was a bit blue in the face by now. It was with difficulty that he spoke, but the words were somehow gasped out. 'You get one.'

Dave let him go at that. The saloon-keeper, no lightweight himself, rubbed his throat and looked at a sawn-off shot gun back of the bar, and then he went and sat down and leaned on a table and tried to get his strength back.

He had never met a man with such awful strength in his fingers. He said to no one in particular: 'I reckon that Texan could lick a gorilla if he tried. Reckon he could lick that crazy wrestler if ever he met up with him.'

Dave knew nothing about any crazy wrestler, but he wasn't interested in compliments just then. He went round to the saloon stables and picked himself a good bay gelding. It was quite dark when he rode out on to the main street, a street illuminated now only by the lamps in the clapboard buildings that made up Scalping Knife. Even so, a lot of the men were still getting their horses together and their kit upon their horses, preparatory to an expedition which might take more than a few hours.

Dave had little idea of where he was going when he came out of the stable on that big, rangey bay. All he knew was that Scalping Knife was an unhealthy place, and it might be as well for him to be out of the town before sunrise. He thought about joining the men who were going out to find the Indians who had committed the reputed massacre, and then he changed his mind.

He didn't like mobs. More, there were men in that mob who mightn't like him and might take an opportunity of putting lead into his back if they had a chance. He was thinking of the supporters of both the Missouri Mauler and Ontario's pride, Lecleux. There would be some who wouldn't forgive him for thrashing the pair in one day.

Abruptly he halted. A man had come out of a store along the street. He was carrying a sack of provisions, which he threw over the back of his horse and then mounted. The yellow light fell upon a lean face under a wide-brimmed hat.

Dave, on an impulse, spurred forward and crowded that rider into an alley. He heard a startled exclamation from the man. 'What the — '

Dave had recognized him. It was one of the three men who had taken in that dying old man who had made the town with his last strength.

Now he used forceful tactics, suspicion rampant in his mind. He knew this man was up to something, knew that he and his companions had stirred up the town for some purpose of their own.

He didn't know how he knew it. It was just a hunch, but the Texan paid heed to hunches.

That startled rider found himself gripped by the shirt front. He heard a voice say in the darkness, 'Brother, you've got a lot of questions to answer.'

The man felt himself in the grip of a strength far greater than his own, and he made not the slightest attempt to struggle. His eyes instead probed the blackness behind the shadowy outline of his unknown adversary.

Dave rapped, 'What's behind all this? Where are you goin'? How come you didn't ride off with them other galoots that you got all het up?'

The man snarled, 'Let go, darn yer. I got no answers to give to them questions. I don't know what you're talkin' about.'

Dave said, 'I'll bet you do. I'll bet it's something to do with that old man you took in. Now, talk, or I'll shake the teeth out of your head.'

He gave a mild shake. Mild, according to big Dave Oak, but it nearly broke the neck of his adversary.

Even then the fellow made no resistance. Instead Dave realized that his eyes were desperately searching beyond him. And then all at once, even as Dave watched, there was a quick light of satisfaction momentarily gleaming in those eyes.

Dave threw the man to the ground. Simultaneously, even as he hurled himself off his horse, instinct guiding him, a gun blatted flame close to him, lighting up that shadowy alleyway. The bullet spanged into the woodwork just about level with Dave's head, and smashed a plank in two.

When Dave hit the ground, his guns were out and he was firing under the belly of that bay gelding which went into a panic and reared and kicked and nearly knocked the daylight out of Dave's adversary.

Dave's guns jumped in his hands as he triggered lead towards those gouting flames. He heard a yell, and then the clang of metal, and knew he had shot a gun out of an unseen opponent's hand.

Then he jumped after his own horse. He caught it in the act of plunging out towards the mesquite. By the time he'd swung into the saddle and fought the crazy beast to a standstill, his late adversary had swung on to his horse and departed at a gallop down the main street, followed by two other riders.

Dave circled his horse in the darkness of the mesquite for a few minutes, letting its fears quieten, until it became tractable and easy under his grip again. It was blowing and had come out in a lather of sweat, but Dave knew it would suffer no harm because of it. He looked back towards the lighted buildings of that sprawling little town, still undecided what to do or where to go. And then, without really thinking of his actions, he steered his horse towards that end building where an old man was dying or dead, and his daughter would be grieving.

Dave felt that he wanted to see that girl again. He felt that he would like to comfort her in her grief.

He approached softly, his horse making little sound in the sandy waste that backed on to the building. He loomed up out of the night, a shadowy horseman on a shadowy horse. His head was bent forward, peering, but it was not for moments that he made out the rear of this darkened building.

Then he realized that on the steps leading up to the back porch someone was silently sitting. He stiffened, his hands instinctively reaching for his guns. And then he relaxed.

Quietly he swung down from his mount and left it to nibble at whatever it could find. Dave walked slowly forward.

The girl was sitting huddled in misery on those steps. She didn't see him approach, her grief blinding her to everything.

When he got near, Dave made out her face as a pale oval in the faint light that came from a gaming establishment's windows. There was a glisten on that face which told of tears. Dave's heart melted. He wanted to reach out and take this girl in his arms and help her over her grief.

Instead he came to within a foot of her and then squatted on his heels and shoved back his hat and waited for her to speak.

Probably she didn't recognize him. She just sat crying silently, her face lifted to a starlit sky, her grief so great that she didn't care who witnessed it.

Dave's voice welled up in a low rumble of sound that was meant to be sympathetic. He said, 'Your pop's — dead?'

He could have bitten his tongue for using that word, but it came out. The girl said nothing but wept on. That was his answer.

Dave unhappily sifted dry sand through his fingers, and then he couldn't go away without speaking again, so he said, 'You'll get over it.'

And then he said, 'I'd like to help you get over it.'

Just silence from that girl. He despaired. It was as if she was deaf to his voice.

He rose to his feet, and he looked mountain-sized in that darkness. He tried again. 'I know you don't like me. I'm a fighter. That's what you think I am, anyway — a fighter. But it's the truth I'm telling you. I was pushed into that fight with a gun.'

She didn't move. He went on.

'I wish you wouldn't cry. I wish you'd speak to me. Believe me, I'd be a mighty proud man if I could help you now.'

After a half-minute's silence he turned and went back to his horse. His heart was like lead. She didn't want to have anything to do with him.

Yet from the horse he found himself saying, 'I could look after you. If you've got no one in this town to look after you, I figger you ought to have someone. I could do it.'

He got on to his horse. There was no use staying when a fellow wasn't wanted, he was thinking. He even wheeled his horse preparatory to heading out across the mesquite, and then he heard the rush of sudden movement behind him.

He felt someone grip his stirrup. He looked down and saw the girl's pale face, tear-stained and anguished, looking up at his. He heard her voice saying, 'Oh, don't go, Please! I do need someone. I haven't anyone to turn to. And you sound so kind.'

Dave never remembered coming out of that saddle. All he knew was that suddenly he was standing before her, his hat twiddling between his big brown fingers. He looked into a face that was appealing to him for help now, where before it had seemed unheeding of his proffered assistance. She was crying. 'I haven't anyone to look after me. I shan't have anywhere to go. My money's just about run out. Dad told me to wait for his return and then we'd have plenty of money.'

She broke down then, at the thought of her father. Dave put his arm around her shoulders and walked her back to the steps. Now suddenly he was in control of himself and the situation. He knew what to do and what to say.

He said, 'I want you to tell me about your dad. I figger things have been happening that need investigating. How come he came staggering in from the mesquite, done in and dying?'

'He went looking for a fortune,' the girl answered dully. Her face lifted and her eyes met Dave's. 'He spoke a little to me before he died. He kept saying they had found what they set out to find, and he said that as he was the last survivor it was all his and therefore mine if he died.'

Dave asked gently, 'What's all yours? And how do you find it?'

'The reward's mine,' was the girl's answer. And then she pulled herself together. She said, 'This doesn't make sense to you, does it?'

He smiled and she saw the flash of his teeth in the darkness. He said, in that drawling voice of his, 'It don't make much sense, I'll admit, ma'am.'

She said, quickly, 'Please — won't you call me Sue?'

He nodded. 'Sue,' he amended.

She told him the story. It was a curious story she had to tell, too. It was a story of a treasure hunt and yet with an unusual treasure.

'It began over the registration of mine claims up in the Round Hills country,' she began. 'There was a lot of trouble over claims up there, and so they were marked out and registered anew by a Government surveyor.

'One of the men in the Round Hills said he'd been cheated out of a promising claim, and by all accounts it sent him a little crazy.'

Dave said: 'That's the second crazy galoot I've heard mentioned tonight.'

The girl went on with her story. 'This crazy miner, Jud Wheelan, decided to have his revenge. If he had lost his claim, then he would see that nobody else had title to any claim, either.'

'So?'

'In his madness he lay in wait for the surveyor, riding to the county town with the deeds establishing the miners' claims. The crazy miner shot him dead, and then made off with the leather bag containing the title deeds.'

Big young Dave Oak looked down on to that pale oval face, all he could see even in the faint starlight. He exclaimed, 'Now, what'n heck was the good of that?'

Sue sighed. 'Nobody knew. All they knew was that Jud Wheelan was a quarrelsome man, ever fighting, and this last act of craziness was quite in keeping with his character.'

He said: 'Killing that surveyor was murder. That would make him an outlaw.'

'Yes.' Sue nodded in the darkness. 'He went off to try to join up with the Indians, so people said — '

'The Snakes?' Dave was surprised.

The Snakes was the local name for the Shoshone Indians, fierce warriors who would not show friendship towards any white man.

'But apparently they wouldn't have anything to do with him,' Sue continued, 'and he's been ranging the hills alone since his crime.'

'And the title deeds?' asked Dave shrewdly, guessing them to be at the root of all this bother.

'Jud Wheelan hid them somewhere, and boasted about it one time when he'd held up a store for provisions. Apparently he couldn't bring himself about to destroy those deeds, and it tickled his crazy sense of humour to have people go out and search for them.'

'An' people did?'

Again Sue nodded. 'A lot of them. You see, with the surveyor dead and their claims to land lost with those deeds, it set up a lot of claim jumping in the mining area. Nobody could call any land his own, and it led to an outbreak of crime, including murder.'

'I c'n imagine it,' said Dave, grimly. 'An' what did they do about it?'

'A reward was offered by a number of mine-owners totalling ten thousand dollars for the recovery of those deeds. That was why so many parties went out to try to find them.'

'Your father was one of them?'

'He set off a couple of weeks back with three companions. He guessed where Jud Wheelan might have hidden the deeds, because once Jud had been on a hunting party with him, and had shown him a secret cache where he stored meat over the winter. It was in the Laramie Range.' Her voice broke a little. 'By what my father told me in his delirium, his hunch turned out right. They found the bag containing the deeds.'

Dave gave her time to recover, then asked gently: 'What happened to them?'

'When they started to ride out with the deeds they ran into an ambush set by Shoshones. They lost their horses, and had to trek out on foot. They couldn't carry that clumsy mail bag, so they hid it again.'

Quickly: 'Did your father say where he had hidden it?'

'No. I'm afraid he wasn't very coherent. I only picked up this story from stray snatches of words in his delirium. Apparently they had a very bad time of it. Ben, one of the party, and one of Dad's oldest friends, was severely wounded and held them back. They were without water, and that proved worse than the Indians.'

Dave asked: 'Who were with him in the party?'

'The only one I knew was my father's friend, Ben Eden. They picked up a big cattle-puncher who had come to Wyoming for horses, and there was another man whose name was Tuff Leech, I believe.'

She frowned, but he didn't see that in the darkness. 'I didn't like Tuff Leech much.' And then she checked herself. 'I'm sorry, it isn't good to speak ill of the dead.'

'An' they're all dead?'

'Dad said so in a lucid moment before he died.' She tried to remember that moment, though it was painful to her. 'Dad tried so hard to give me a message before he finally collapsed and — and died.

'He kept saying: 'It's all yours now, Sue'. That's how it was arranged. If anyone survived the whole reward went to him. 'I'm the last to survive. It's mine, and if I hand in my chips it comes to you'.'

She broke down then, her shoulders heaving. She didn't want to have any reward. All she wanted was that bold adventurous father of hers to be alive again.

Dave could only sit and listen to her weeping in the darkness. He wanted to put his arm round her and comfort her, but he knew he hadn't known her long enough for that. Deliberately he kept her talking about the expedition, however, partly because a little hunch was growing in his mind, and also because he felt that by keeping her thoughts on it he would be diverting them from the loss of her father.

'You know,' he said in that slow drawling voice of his, 'I figgered them three galoots was up to no good. The three who took your Dad in,' he explained.

'You mean Deevan, Hewitt and Ed Scholls?' He nodded, guessing those to be the men he was referring to.

'They were a mighty long time attending to your father in this hut before comin' out an' broadcastin' the information that he was back in town,' Dave said grimly. 'My guess is they were listenin' in on his ravin's, tryin' to piece together the story, just like you did. I reckon they weren't concerned that he was dyin', only that he had a secret that was worth ten thousand dollars to them.

'I guess they learnt that secret, and when they'd got it they lit out to find them deeds.' His voice was grim. It wasn't going to be pleasant for Deevan, Hewitt and Ed Scholls if ever Dave Oak met up with them.

Sue was puzzled. 'But why did they rouse the town and get them riding westward?'

Dave wrinkled his nose and thought that one out. 'I reckon they figgered Shoshone territory was mighty unhealthy for any small group of white men. So cunningly they got the townspeople out to keep the Shoshones occupied while they looked for the title deeds.'

His eyes were intent on a spot in the darkness. Something had moved.

Sue didn't realize that his attention was diverted, and she went on, 'But how could they know where the deeds were hidden? I don't think my father was lucid enough to explain to anyone.'

Dave's hand was on his gun. Yet part of his mind sought the answer to this question. He was remembering something. To himself he was saying, 'Four men went on that expedition. An' that was a quarter of a dollar I saw strung around the old man's neck. That's how it would be, I guess.'

Aloud he said; 'Did you find a quarter-dollar strung around your father's neck?'

He knew what the answer would be. 'No.' The girl's voice was wondering. 'There was nothing strung round his neck. Why do you ask?'

And then she was surprised, because big Dave was rising very slowly and for the first time she grasped the significance of that movement of his hand towards his gun.

Dave was still speaking, and she wasn't to know that that was to make whoever it was out there careless, to let them think they hadn't been detected.

'I guess they did an old trick, your father and his buddies. I reckon when they hid that bag they marked the spot and recorded the position on a silver dollar which they broke into four pieces.'

'I see,' said the girl quickly. 'That means that until someone secures possession of all four pieces no one will be able to find the hiding-place of those deeds?'

Dave nodded. 'That's my guess, too. I reckon Deevan an' his pards got that silver quarter from your Dad an' rode off to look for the other three quarters.' And then he added, 'I reckon that's what I'm goin' to do at first light myself, too.'

And then suddenly something launched itself at him unexpectedly. In a second he found himself fighting for his life against something that was as hard to grasp as a snake.

4

Blue — All Over!

Dave hadn't expected that attack, and his gun wasn't clear of its holster when that form cannoned into him. He let go of his gun and put up his hands to protect himself.

They met naked skin — skin covered with something greasy upon which his fingers slipped and failed to find a hold. At the same time savage hands clawed at his throat, and he heard a snarl that was more bestial than human as he went crashing down on to the hard-baked ground. He heard Sue scream with terror, and then he began to roll, fighting for his life.

It was a weird struggle, rolling on the ground, fighting an unknown opponent of incredible strength. Dave found, too, that he was opposed to a man with enormous reach — a reach greater than his own, so that there was a danger of being throttled without being able to get at his opponent in defence.

So Dave began to roll. That way his opponent had to go with him or release his hold. The opponent hung on and Dave's efforts dragged the slippery body over the top of him. Then Dave lashed out into the darkness and made contact with an unseen head. He knew it hurt. He felt the grip on his throat relax at once.

Gasping, he kicked himself away and came staggering to his feet. That snarling opponent came launching like an arrow at his throat again. There was something curiously snake-like in the way that lean, lithe figure came darting in. By this time Dave was ready and smashed out with a mighty right that connected with ribs and must have nearly caved them in.

The snarling opponent went staggering away into the darkness.

Dave gave his unknown attacker no

respite. Raging at the cowardly attack from the darkness, the big Texas puncher hurled his mighty weight after that shadowy shape.

He caught up with him reeling round a corner. Even in that darkness Dave had an impression of immense height, of something thin, sinuous, and snake-like. He was also suddenly conscious that his hands felt greasy after contact with that slimy body.

For a few hectic seconds the two fought it out madly in the darkness. Dave never said a word, but the unknown opponent hissed and snarled like some cornered animal.

Then Dave found himself staggering as a lucky blow caught him off his balance. He went rolling frantically into the dust, to make distance between himself and his opponent.

But his attacker had had enough. In fact, his attacker had had more than enough. He must have been a very surprised man to find he had picked on anyone so redoubtable as Dave Oak.

Dave came clawing up to his knees, only to find that his enemy had gone. Someone ran into him in the darkness, and he turned swiftly and grabbed. Hands beat at his face, and he heard the quick breathing of someone in a high state of agitation. His hands were so greasy that they didn't hold those slim wrists and they broke away and beat at him again.

So Dave went on the retreat, laughing a little and calling out warningly, 'Hey, Sue, that's no way to treat your friend!'

Sue stopped striking at him immediately. He heard her gasp with relief.

'Oh, Dave,' she exclaimed. 'When you grabbed me, I — I thought it was that other — thing!'

Dave was surprised she used that word. It jerked him erect. Because he, too, had had an uncanny feeling that he had fought against something not quite human.

He said, 'It was mighty plucky of you to come and try to help me, Sue.' He took her by the elbow, watching around into the shadowy darkness all the time, and steered her back to where the light from one of the buildings streamed out towards them. He was feeling very uncomfortable.

As they came up on to the porch and fully into that light he heard Sue gasp and realized that she was staring at him. He exclaimed, 'What's the matter, Sue?'

She said, 'You're blue, Dave — blue all over!'

Dave looked down at himself and then spread his hands and looked at them. He was mystified. He seemed to be covered with a blue grease that was over all his clothes and his hands.

'What'n heck — ' he exclaimed. His mind immediately began to race.

His eyes lifted and looked at Sue. She was staring at him in wonder, not understanding.

Slowly Dave said, 'I remember now, somethin' your father said when they were carryin' him in. He was ravin' about a blue Injun.'

He saw the light leap into Sue's blue eyes. She exclaimed, 'Dad was talking about that Indian in his delirium, just before he died. He was in fear, it seemed, and I thought it was just some kind of nightmare, some delirium. He seemed to be trying to get away from this Indian, and he kept saying that he was the only one of his companions to have escaped him.'

Things were fitting together. Dave said slowly, 'I've never heard of a blue Injun. But I'm beginnin' to see how things are.'

His mind went back to that missing silver quarter. He was thinking that those other quarters would be on the bodies of the three adventurers who had accompanied old Ezra Hallet, and then he thought, 'Mebbe that's why the Injun followed Ezra right out here. Mebbe he knows about them quarters an' he wants to collect 'em for himself.'

That didn't sound like an Indian, but at least it explained why that relentless pursuer should be lurking in the vicinity of where Ezra Hallet lay.

Sue said, practically, 'You'd better go and get that stuff cleaned off you. I'll be waiting for you here when you come back.'

Dave began to go away off that porch, and then he smiled back at the girl. He called, 'Don't move out of this light, Sue, and if you think there's goin' to be any more trouble, just fire this off an' I'll come a-runnin'.'

She found a Colt pushed into her hand. She went and sat on a chair and he saw the light upon her fair head as he retreated down the main street in search of a saloon where he could wash.

He came back in a hurry, with a feeling that this wonderful girl might have gone in the short time of his absence, and it was with considerable relief that he saw her still sitting there. During that short time, too, he had made up his mind.

He said to her, 'What are you going to do?'

She looked at him helplessly. 'I don't know. I haven't any money, and I don't think there's work for me in a town like this. I only came to look after my father. Now he's gone I'd better move back east and — and start life over again.'

Her eyes were watching the big Texan as she spoke. Dave wanted to say, 'You stay around here, Sue Hallet. I'll look after you!'

That was how he was feeling even after this short time. But he knew that he couldn't speak like that.

But he did say, 'Y'know what your father said. That you're the heir to what his party found.'

'But they didn't bring in those deeds and so claim the reward,' she pointed out.

'Nope. But we know they found them, an' it seems to me it wouldn't be difficult to get them quarters an' find out where your father an' his pards hid the stuff again.'

His eyes were looking beyond the girl now, calculating. He was thinking that three crooks were already on the trail of those missing quarters — and they had the first quarter in their possession. It would mean going after those crooks and taking that quarter away from them for a start. That didn't frighten the big Texan. His mind was being made up in those seconds.

He spoke again. 'Sue, that's what I'm goin' to do for you. I'm goin' on the trail of them missin' quarters, an' I'm goin' to find that bag of deeds. I'm goin' to bring it in for you an' you can claim that ten thousand dollar reward an' you'll be settled for life.'

She didn't jump for joy at his words. Instead, he saw the frown on her pretty face, and the look of anxiety in her eyes. He heard her say, 'I don't want you to go after those deeds, Dave. They've brought enough trouble as it is!'

She turned away quickly so that he couldn't see her emotion as she was reminded again of her father so recently dead. Dave spoke to her back. 'All the same, Sue, I'm goin' after them deeds. I ain't gonna let no passel o' crooks get away with what your father gave his life for. They're rightly yours, for you to claim the reward, an' I'm lightin' out at daybreak on the trail.'

* * *

Daybreak. Dave was already a few miles along the trail, knowing the way the old man must have come in. There was only one ford on the river that a weakened man could negotiate and he went straight towards it. He splashed through the shadows in the brilliant early-morning sunshine, and he felt content with the world.

He was mounted on a fine horse again. He was embarking on a desperate adventure, but one which suited his temperament. And he had found the most wonderful girl in the world and he was riding now to help her.

He was content.

He crossed this tributary of the Platte and then cast around for a trail. It was easy to find. Three horsemen paralleled the dragging footprints of a solitary wayfarer. All he had to do was to follow the tracks of those three crooks intent on cheating a girl out of her dues, and he would go back on the trail of Ezra Hallet.

He rode for several hours, and then the tops of tall dark trees showed ahead across the dusty, wind-scoured mesquite. He peered against a rising dust storm towards this other tributary of the Platte.

It was a place where a man might expect an ambush, and big Dave Oak was too trail-wise to take any risks. He went into that long belt of vegetation in a circling movement, a detour that brought him in among the tree belt far to the north of where the trail led. Cautiously he rode back among the trees until he picked up the trail again.

He need not have taken any precautions. Only one man lay there among the grasses in wait for him, and he was dead.

Dave looked round carefully before dismounting, and then, sure that he was alone, he slid out of his saddle and approached that recumbent figure.

He saw a tall, lean man, and by his attire it was obvious that he was a cowboy like himself. He noticed the way both arms were outflung and the fingers dug in death agony into the dry soil. He saw how the man had been brutally struck down from behind.

Kneeling, he examined those wounds. After a while he rose, muttering, 'That was Injun's work!'

It was knife and tomahawk work, he was thinking, and then he pulled back the man's shirt to see if any cord was around his neck. There was no cord. He searched that body but there was no silver quarter on it.

When he had done that he sat on his heels and rolled himself a curly and thought. He thought, 'Someone got away with this poor galoot's quarter.' And he wondered who had taken it — the three crooks who were ahead of him or that blue Indian?

Sitting there provided no answer to his problem, so he searched around until he found loose rock and then he brought them back and piled them in a cairn around that unfortunate cowboy. When that was done he took the trail again.

The tracks of the three men now paralleled two sets of footsteps — old Ezra's and that lanky cowboy's. It was easy to follow the trail, especially when he rode out of the grassland that fringed the tree belt along the tributary. On the mesquite the trail was still very apparent, even though this rising, driving wind was filling in the footprints rapidly with the blowing desert dust. He had to ride now with his head bent towards the storm that hourly grew worse. But he had to go on, this was no time for stopping. He had to keep on this trail before it was obliterated.

He found himself climbing now, and in between lulls in that duststorm he was able to see hills ahead of him and to realize that he was heading into a broad valley between two ranges.

For hours he rode, battling against the gritty storm that made him choke and sweat intolerably. The horse, uncertain with its new master, didn't like that driving wind and continually tried to circle and run with it. It met its match in the big Texan, who fought the beast and kept it going along the disappearing trail marks.

Dave came out where a giant sandstone outcrop reared suddenly in the midst of the mesquite. It provided a shelter from that needling duststorm, but Dave wasn't long enjoying the respite.

Almost the moment he came before those rocks, a shot rang out. He hardly heard the report because of the scream of the wind as it blew around those jagged rock edges, but he heard the vicious hum of the rotating bullet as it whizzed close by his head and he didn't need to be told that he was being shot at.

Instinctively Dave hurled himself off his horse. He had no idea which way his enemy or enemies lay — to ride on was maybe to ride towards a gun muzzle.

As he came out of the saddle he dragged his rifle from its scabbard, and immediately he was on the ground he rolled behind a bush that gave him cover. His horse skittered around nervously at his sudden exit from the saddle, but it wouldn't trot away from the shelter provided by those rocks.

Dave saw a movement. His rifle jumped as he triggered lead. The movement ceased abruptly, but Dave was sure he hadn't made a hit.

Then a stream of bullets came searching for him from a position out in that swirling, dusty waste to his left. Frantically Dave dug himself down into the ground. He must have been protected — just. Those bullets plucked at his hat and touched his shirt but came no nearer to hurting him.

Screwing his eyes against the driving dust, Dave looked for better shelter. He was too insecure, with only this clump of mesquite to cover him. Inch by inch he began to pull himself backwards to where rocks spilled out from the main outcrop. Lead began to follow him all the way.

He winced as each bullet screamed by him, and he used all the care possible to hug that ground so as to present as little target as possible. He was almost into shelter when a ricochet came screaming up from the rocky ground and sent splinters of stone into his face. Blood oozed up immediately from the many little punctures, and it mixed with the sweat and ran into his eyes, so that for the moment he was blind.

Instinctively he dragged himself into cover. Then he cleaned his eyes and mopped his face tenderly. And then, his face grim and set, he lifted his head and sighted along his rifle.

His enemies must have thought him badly hurt, because they were coming along recklessly. He saw three forms dimly outlined in the swirling dust cloud of that raging storm. His rifle jumped. One of the men screamed — the sound just floated to Dave's ears — and he saw the galoot perform a brief dance and then go crashing down among the mesquite.

'I got one,' Dave thought with satisfaction. Not dead, or he wouldn't have made such a row. But hurt, and that put him out of action. Now he had two enemies to face.

But those two enemies were suddenly cautious again, and with caution they were able to get on top in this little skirmish. Two rifles can always cover a man better than one can cover two.

The fire grew so hot that Dave found himself not even daring to lift his head to return the fire. Every time he moved, lead spanged close to him.

Uneasily he realized that the angle of the shots was changing, and that meant they were crawling close up to him.

He thought, 'It's them three. I caught up with 'em. They must suspect why

I'm trailin' 'em.'

His only chance was to let them think he was still crouched behind those rocks while he made a getaway. He began to crawl behind the cover, in the hope of flanking his enemies.

He had gone a dozen yards, when he realized that almost by his nose as he sidled round a boulder was a man's boot.

He froze, and then he realized an important thing. That was, that during this fight this unseen man had had chance to shoot him down from behind while he fought his enemies. Acting on a hunch, Dave continued round that boulder. He found himself staring at a man who was obviously dead.

Dave's immediate thought was, 'This is another of Ezra Hallet's party.' Quickly he searched that old man who had been dead for more than a day now. There was no cord around his neck with a silver quarter attached to it. And there was no silver quarter in his pocket. Dave thought, 'Someone got here before me.'

He wondered if Deevan, Hewitt and Scholls had found that silver quarter. And then his thoughts raced to that other mysterious figure on the trail of the broken silver dollar, that blue snake-like Indian.

Dave shrugged. He began to crawl again. He had to get round that pair if he were to turn the tables on them.

A minute later he realized that it was impossible. He realized that these tumbling rocks ended here and there was no further cover across the mesquite. He was trapped behind this low wall of rocks. All they had to do was sit out there and wait until thirst and starvation drove him on to their guns.

He rolled on to his side and looked to where his horse was standing fifty yards away with its back to the storm. All his food and water was on that animal — and it might just as well have been a thousand miles away as those fifty yards.

Grimly he raised himself, determined to make a fight of it. His rifle blazed, and he nearly took the hand off one of his enemies. But the only trouble was that he had now betrayed his position again, and after that he could not move for fear of bullets searching him out.

'I'm in a heck of a bad way,' Dave thought wryly. He lay there, enduring that storm and trying not to notice the agonising thirst that grew so quickly in those desert wastes. Once or twice, deliberately he jumped up and took a swift shot, but that was only to make his enemies cautious.

Most of the time he just lay there and wondered how long it would be before the end —

There was a sudden scream from out along the mesquite. Dave stiffened, hearing it, because it was a cry of mortal terror. He heard shots, and then again there was that awful scream.

It might be a ruse to get him to expose himself, he thought grimly, but he couldn't lie there and not know what was going on beyond this rocky cover. He lifted himself cautiously and peered out.

He was in time to see a figure disappear into the dust. All he saw was the semblance of a human form, of a shadowy shape that dissolved almost instantly into the swirling dust.

Dave waited. Nothing happened. He lifted his head another inch. No shot rang out. He came up higher, his eyes searching, yet still nothing happened.

So finally he stood up and no one took a pot at him.

His enemies were no longer to be feared.

With infinite caution, running swiftly from cover to cover, bent almost double so as to present as little target as possible, Dave ran out among those bushes of the mesquite. Suddenly he saw Jeff Deevan.

He didn't know it was Jeff Deevan, but that was the name that corpse had borne until a few minutes before.

Deevan was dead, and Dave didn't

have to know the manner of his death. He had been tomahawked from behind as he lay in those bushes awaiting a movement from his enemy, Dave Oak.

Dave crouched and looked around, but saw no sign of life other than his own horse huddled up against those tall rocks. He scouted around and saw a boot and trousered leg behind a bush.

He didn't have to know the man was dead before he got across to him. It was Ed Scholls, though again Dave wasn't to know it.

By the look of it, Scholls had been trying to scramble away from something that had reared out of the bushes after him. The tomahawk had got him from behind and he was very much dead.

Dave scouted around and found tracks and followed them. A few minutes later he found Hewitt, that injured man, huddled in a dried-up watercourse. When Hewitt saw big Dave Oak his expression changed to one of tremendous relief. No longer was Dave Oak an enemy in the eyes of Hewitt!

Dave dragged him out of that gully and he was babbling like a man demented. He had seen what had happened to Scholls and Deevan.

He had gone away when Dave's shot had shattered his shoulder, but he hadn't gone far out of the fight. He had tried to patch up his wound, and it was while he was so engaged that suddenly he had caught a movement among the bushes right behind Jeff Deevan.

'I thought there was something wrong with my eyes,' Hewitt shuddered. 'I thought I was looking at a snake writhing its way through those bushes. It was long and thin and as blue as the sky above.'

That wasn't a good simile, because there was no sky above during that dust storm. Nevertheless, Dave nodded patiently, understanding.

He saw Hewitt lick his thick lips and noted the abject fear in the man's brown eyes. Hewitt had passed through a moment of the most awful terror.

'I couldn't make out what it was, but before I could reach my gun or shout a warning, I saw that thing jump on to Deevan and kill him. I saw Ed look round and then begin to run, and he was screaming like a man insane!'

Dave had heard those screams. He understood.

'That blue devil was on to him like a flash. Poor Ed never stood a chance!' Hewitt shuddered, remembering the horror of that moment. 'When he'd done for Ed and Jeff I just lay here doggo. I wasn't in any condition to bring that blue devil on to me!'

Dave reached forward and examined the wounded man. They were enemies no longer. He bandaged him roughly and then told Hewitt he could go when he'd answered a few questions.

Hewitt was ready to answer all the questions Dave shot at him.

Sure they'd tumbled to the secret of that silver quarter around old Hallet's neck. Sure they'd gone out to find the other three quarters.

But things hadn't panned out at all right.

Hewitt was in pain, and he was talkative in something of a hysterical manner. Probably but for his wound he would have been sullen, but now plainly he regarded Dave Oak as more an ally than an enemy. He was still scared of that vicious, leaping blue figure, and was all too conscious of his own disability.

Dave prompted him with questions to get the information he wanted. They'd robbed old Hallet of the silver quarter? Hewitt nodded, his eyes squinting against the driving storm, nervously looking for that blue Indian to appear.

'We came out lookin' for them other three quarters,' he admitted. 'It looked a good way of gettin' some money quickly!'

Dave said drily: 'Sure, it was a good way. It didn't matter to you that if anyone was legally entitled to get them deeds and the reward that went with 'em, it was Hallet's daughter!'

Hewitt didn't say anything to that. Plainly he wanted to keep the subject away from his guilt.

He said: 'But we met nothin' but bad luck. We found that dead puncher, and someone had been at him afore us. Leastways, he didn't have no silver quarter on him.'

His eyes switched towards that wall of rock behind which Dave had been crouching.

'Did you see that fellar?' His head indicated the body lying behind the rocks.

Dave said: 'You mean old Ben Eden?' He made a guess at the dead man's identity, but it seemed he was right.

'Ben Eden.' He fumbled and brought out a plug and tore off a chunk with his teeth. His hands were trembling. 'Someone had been there afore us, too. Someone got away with them silver quarters.' He spat brown tobacco juice into the dust. Bad temper showed for an instant. 'Doggone it, it ought to have been easy! Jest ride back along the trail an' pick silver quarters off'n dead bodies! But we was too late!'

Dave rose, standing with his head bent to keep his hat brim shielding his cheek from the needling pieces of sand that came on the tearing wind.

He said: 'I figger you ought to get back to town, fellar. You've got a wound there that won't get better if this dust shifts into it!'

Hewitt didn't want to ride alone. He was grateful for getting off so easily, but he had an unholy dread of the darkness represented by the swirling duststorm back of them. He wanted to stay near to this big, capable-looking man, with the well-worn Colts in his belt.

But Dave wouldn't listen to Hewitt's pleas for company. He had urgent work on hand and intended to get on with it. He had found two of the bodies. Now he must find the third along that dead man's trail.

Roughly he told Hewitt to find his

horse and get on his way. Then he began to march across to where the dust was foaming over the clothes and bodies of Jeff Deevan and Ed Scholl.

Hewitt got his horse and rode off at a mad gallop, as if all the devils in creation were hard on his heels. As he wheeled past Dave, the Texan heard the wounded man shout: 'You must be crazy, riskin' your life here! Ain't you scared?'

Squatting on his heels, rolling the inevitable cigarette, Dave looked after the flying heels of Hewitt's mount and thought: 'Sure, I'm scared!' But he wasn't going to give up this trail just because of some blue devil of an Indian.

He was careful as he searched those bodies — careful at all times to have one hand clasped around his rifle, while his eyes looked more often into the duststorm around him than at the objects of his search.

But no evil, leaping form materialized. Dave got a feeling that the blue

Indian had departed from the vicinity, if only temporarily.

He searched Deevan and then walked across and performed a similar task on Scholl. But no quarter was revealed. If Deevan had had old man Hallet's quarter, as Hewitt declared, then someone had robbed him of it after death.

Thinking about it, Dave sat for a long time on his heels, trying to fit together pieces in this puzzle. All he could think was that that blue Indian was trying to collect these quarters for his own purpose. He couldn't understand why. But the opinion came to him strongly now that probably the blue Indian had all or most of the quarters with the death of Deevan.

He got to his feet, leaning against that powerful wind. He was thinking: 'Looks like I've got to find that blue devil an' try an' get them quarters from him.' By what he knew of the Indian that wasn't going to be easy.

Now he went across and looked again

at that old man lying in the dust behind the rocks. This time he was able to give the body a more thorough examination. He found no silver quarter upon the body, even as he had failed to find it upon his first search, but he did make one important discovery.

Ben Eden hadn't died from a knife or a tomahawk. A bullet had been the cause of his slow death.

And that bullet had been fired into his body from behind.

5

Recognition

When Dave was through with his examination, he walked to where his horse was standing, head down away from the blast. He was in the act of mounting, when some instinct warned him and he turned to look swiftly around.

In some magical manner it seemed that all in one second the earth had erupted figures — the figures of Indians mounted upon small, wiry ponies.

Dave's eyes widened with shock. He hadn't expected this sudden appearance of a hunting party. But standing there in a silent, menacing arc around him were at least a dozen braves. They had arrows strung to their bows and those deadly points were aimed towards him.

The duststorm lifted for a second and he saw the war-paint on those grim-faced blanketed Indians. They were Shoshones — Snakes!

Dave lifted his rifle like a flash. He wasn't going to let himself be cut down without a struggle or, worse still, taken prisoner by this ferocious tribe of Indians.

The Shoshones had lived farther west and south of this locality until the United States army had driven them off their hunting grounds which were across the new trails into the gold-producing areas of California and Nevada. The Shoshones were now deadly enemies of all white men, and Dave knew what horrible fate awaited him if he fell into their hands.

His rifle thundered and a bullet went leaping towards one of those Indians. Simultaneously something fell on him — something of weight that smashed him to the ground. Almost in that same moment a stunning blow descended upon his skull and his consciousness began to ebb swiftly away from him.

He could only think, 'Them Injuns were waitin' for me to come back for my hoss. One of them varmints must have been lurkin' on top of the rocks.'

That Indian had struck him to the ground and given him this knock-out blow —

When Dave came to consciousness it was to a realization of an agony so tremendous it seemed for a long time insupportable.

He realized that he was slung across a nimble-footed Indian pony, belly down upon a sweaty bare back. He was tied by his wrists to his ankles under the gaunt ribs of that pony. His position, combined with the wound on his head resulting from that swift, savage blow was painful to a degree. He felt as if his head would burst.

His thirst was agonizing, too, but he had to lie there and make the best of it. No one offered him a drink. No one tried to ease his position over the back of that trotting pony.

After a time the throbbing in his skull diminished a little and he was able to take some interest in his surroundings. By twisting his neck awkwardly he was able to see the legs of the other ponies accompanying his own. He could also see the bare limbs and feet of his Indian captors. The duststorm appeared to be dying now, and for that at any rate he was grateful.

He realized that his own fine bay gelding was being ridden by one of the Indians.

They rode all that afternoon until close on darkness, and then they arrived by a stream and began to make a primitive camp. Plainly the Indians were alert for trouble. No doubt they had been part of the Shoshone tribe routed in battle by the Scalping Knife settlers earlier that afternoon.

Now they were fleeing deeper into the wilderness in an effort to escape the white man's vengeance.

All this Dave understood without a word being spoken to him. But he also realized that defeated Indians weren't generous captors. It was going to be very hard when they turned their attentions towards him. In spite of his courage, Dave Oak was pale, lying on the ground where they had thrown him. The Shoshones had a brand of torture that made men shudder throughout the length and breadth of America.

He was working on the thongs made of deerhide that tied him, but he knew it was hopeless. Thongs were more efficient than rope. A thong had a degree of elasticity that rendered movement of the wrists almost impossible. After a time Dave gave up the struggle. If he were to escape it would only be because someone came and helped him.

He managed to sit up in the dust, watching the lengthening shadows and the preparations for camp. He thought to himself, 'Where have I a friend who can help me out here in this wilderness?'

The Indians weren't lighting any fire.

They would probably do that after darkness, when ascending smoke wouldn't betray their position, and when they could screen their tiny cooking fire from the view of any possible hostile eyes.

For the moment the Indians were content to fill their bellies with much needed water and then to lie in the shade and rest.

But while they rested silently those fierce Indian faces never left their captive's. He could read in their eyes his impending doom, and he could tell by their manner that the way out was not going to be easy for him.

The Indians had posted a couple of sentries far out, and very soon, after they got down to rest, one brave came loping in, clearly bearing news of an enemy in the vicinity.

Dave didn't know the Shoshone tongue, and he could only listen to it without understanding.

In time, though, it became apparent that these Indians had been made uneasy by the report of the returning sentry. They sat up after that, their hands on their weapons, their eyes anxiously looking out over the darkening landscape.

As darkness descended upon the resting men, it became increasingly evident to the watchful Dave Oak that the Indians were under a heightening tension. It was not understandable to him. This was not the sort of conduct he expected of Shoshones.

True, they weren't as fanatically reckless and savage as the Comanche of his native Texas, neither were they as soldierly as the Cheyenne Nation.

But all the same the Shoshones were one of the most intrepid warrior tribes among the redskins. Yet here he saw them in evident fear.

One thing he knew. These Indians weren't showing this fear because of white men. An Indian would go out to meet death without showing fear if his enemy were one of the hated palefaces. Yet they were afraid.

Suddenly they had more concrete reasons for fear. Away in the dusk of the mesquite, a wild scream rang out. For one second it seemed to soar as if borne on the wings of terror. And then, as if a knife were cut through that scream, it stopped.

Dave tried to struggle into a sitting position because he had heard that scream once before. He thought he understood the significance of it.

The Indians seemed to lose their nerve at that. There was a frantic jabbering of voices, and then recklessly they hurled themselves towards their resting ponies. Even so they did not leave their prisoner behind. They were fleeing from their unknown terror and yet they would not give up their hated paleface prisoner.

Once again Dave found himself roughly slung across the back of a pony. This time they didn't tie him on, but bound as he was he knew better than to try to roll off the pony's back.

He guessed that an Indian lance

would be through his back in an instant if he made such an attempt to escape.

As they sped off into the night Dave could only think grimly, 'I've got myself into one heck of a position!'

Whatever happened, it seemed things would be just too bad for the big Texan. If only he could get his hands free, he thought despairingly, but those Indians had made sure of the bonds that held him.

He noticed one significant thing. They left behind them the ponies of the two sentries out on watch. He understood why.

Neither sentry would return from his post.

Now he understood the first agitation. That sentry must have loped back into the camp to tell of the disappearance of his comrade. Or perhaps he had even found him lying dead.

Now that other sentry had been struck down and his scream had warned as well as panicked his comrades.

Lying across that jolting, uncomfortable horse, Dave could only think, 'It won't do 'em any good. They can't escape!'

Perhaps the Indians knew it, too. Perhaps they sensed that in the darkness that thing was pursuing them. Perhaps they knew about that dreaded blue devil that leapt on them and killed them before they had time to retreat.

Dave screwed his neck so that he could look at the mesquite in that near darkness, but though his eyes searched all the time he never once saw signs of pursuit. Yet he knew that within reach of them, also rode that blue devil —

When complete darkness came they were entering rougher country, ascending from this high mesa, into rolling hills that footed the mighty Laramie Range.

The moon came up almost immediately, and it gave them brilliant light. It helped them in their mad flight westwards, and yet it added to the terror of those demoralized Indians because they knew themselves to be revealed to any silent, ruthless pursuer.

It made the occasional trees and more frequent clumps of bushes take on a ghostly shadowness in that hard, steely light, and within half an hour Dave could sense that those superstitious Indians were about at the end of their mental tether.

Yet still they dragged his horse along. Still they wouldn't give up their prisoner.

They would hang on to him until the bitter end, thought Dave, and it wasn't consoling to think of that end. He would die under the torture of the Shoshone squaw-women.

After a couple of hours their horses began to blow out. They were climbing now, and it was so cold that they were shivering. One of the leaders, less panic-stricken than the others, shouted for a halt. With much fear the Indians grouped together, huddling close to each other for protection and also for the warmth that rose from the steaming bodies of their ponies.

They faced outwards, with their prisoner still slung across his horse in their midst, and their eyes watched the grey horizon on all sides of them.

Nothing moved.

Half an hour later and still nothing had moved. By this time something like courage had returned to those warriors. Perhaps, too, they felt the shame of their ignominious flight, for it was not usual for a brave to run away from what he feared.

They even grew a little reckless, wanting to prove now that after all they hadn't really been so scared before. They got down and walked about, and then sat down close against some camel thorn bushes, and they even spoke to each other in guttural whispers.

Their courage certainly was coming back. And the longer they sat there without any frightening movement from the mesquite, the higher their spirits mounted.

Still Dave hadn't been pulled off his

horse. Indians never considered the comfort of their prisoners. He could lie like that, and if it was uncomfortable, well, he was a paleface and deserved it.

There came a moment when the leaders of this little party decided that long enough had been spent in resting. The horses were fit for the trail again, and Dave Oak heard sharp commands which clearly indicated that the warriors must mount and ride on.

Only, something curious happened when they were mounted and ready to ride away. The light was good enough for Dave to see and to understand when consternation rose among those Indians.

For two of the ponies were now without riders!

It brought those Indians thrashing round on their ponies, their old mad fears galloping back into their superstitious brains immediately. Two of their party had disappeared while they were sitting together, shoulders almost touching each other.

The flight started again. This was an enemy too formidable for even the bravest of the Shoshones. An enemy who could wriggle in among them and kill and carry away his victims while they sat watching for him was something out of their understanding.

It brought a chill even to Dave Oak's heart. For it seemed dreadful, to be bound and helpless and to know that such an evil, terrifying thing was stalking them.

It was at that moment that he began to reason out the identity of that snake-like blue Indian who followed them. He was no Indian, Dave was thinking!

They had strung out in their flight across the mesquite, and were riding upon each other's hoofs where a winding game trail climbed between close-pressing bushes and small trees. All at once a scream split the night air behind them. A few seconds later a terrified, riderless pony came galloping past them, overtaking them easily because of its fears and because it was without its master's weight.

The thing was striking them down now, even while they rode, and yet looking back they could not see it.

They had climbed a bare shoulder that lifted high above the mesquite and were plunging ever upwards towards the snowy peaks of the Laramie Range. Then Dave Oak's mount stumbled, caught its stride and went on. But that stumble was fatal for Dave Oak — or that's what he thought during that agonized moment when his pony went down on to its knees.

For Dave came hurtling off his mount, and the warriors didn't see him. Or if they did, they weren't waiting to pick him up. They were too terrified now to check their mad flight away from the thing that stalked them.

Dave crashed to the rocky ground, with a jolt that nearly sent him unconscious. For a moment he was sure he had broken every bone in his body, and then, because of his superb fitness and enormous strength, the pain waves receded and he realized that apart from some bruises he had probably suffered no ill effects from that fall.

His heart was thumping. Somehow he rolled on to his side, so that he could look down the trail whence they had come. He was helpless and he knew that in a moment that thing would come out on the trail towards him.

Time passed. A bush stirred. Something moved in the darkness. Then Dave felt a sinister, sliding movement to his rear.

Frantically he rolled. His eyes searched the moonlit ground behind him. Nothing moved.

He was still watching that way when a stealthy sound reached him from close to his head. He kicked and brought himself round, facing it.

There was nothing. Only a shadow beside a bush.

He blinked and when he looked again that shadow wasn't there.

Now he knew that it wasn't imagination that supplied those frightening noises. A shadow had disappeared!

That meant the presence of someone close to him. Snarling to himself now, beads of sweat breaking out from his forehead, Dave somehow got in a sitting position and then somehow swung himself to his knees. He was tied and helpless still, but he felt better, being in an upright position to meet his enemy.

He waited, his head cocked to one side, listening.

Perhaps, though, that movement of his had betrayed the fact that he was helplessly bound. Or perhaps, kneeling like that, it was apparent in the moonlight.

He saw a movement along to his right and his eyes immediately focused on it. The movement grew more pronounced. A shadow detached itself and began to creep silently towards him.

That was all it was at first. A shadow.

Just a black thing that moved slowly, stealthily towards him under that moonlight.

Then, all at once, it was no shadow. Instead Dave looked upon this fierce enemy that attacked white man and red. And he knew him.

He had never met this man before, couldn't recognize in this fierce, blue-painted, death-masked medicine man, anyone he had ever met.

Yet he knew him.

Even as that snake-like figure glided towards his helpless prey, knife and tomahawk gripped for the brutal despatch, Dave called out, 'What's this game you're playin', Jud Whelan!'

6

Tempting Danger

It had its effect, that abrupt shout of the big husky, kneeling in his bonds in the moonlight. That shadowy figure only twenty yards away came to an abrupt halt that spoke of the shock that came with those words.

For one long second the hideous, masked, seven-foot apparition seemed to hang on his heels.

Then once again he came forward, and if there'd been any before, there was no doubt as to his intention now. Jud Whelan, renegade white man and would-be Indian, was going to despatch this man who had seen through his secret. He came in quickly, hurling himself at the foe who had once before defeated him in the night.

Dave saw the moonlight glistening on

that long, snake-like blue form. He saw for one fleeting instant that carved death mask that was worn by a medicine man. And in the bright moonlight those emblems of death around that blue figure's waist — those skulls and human bones — glistened whitely.

But Dave wasn't a man to go under without a fight even though he were bound and helpless. Raging against the bonds which left him so helpless before his savage enemy, Dave threw himself sideways and at the same time lashed out viciously with his bound legs.

Luck was with him. The incredible happened. Probably it happened because that blue Indian who wasn't an Indian — that crazy man who answered to the name of Jud Whelan — didn't think there would be any fight in his adversary. So he came on, over-confident, over-cautious.

Dave had a momentary impression of a flying form sailing over his head as he fell back. He felt the sickening thud as his feet slammed into naked limbs. He heard a gasp of pain from behind that death mask, and then that form continued its flight over and beyond his head, hands outstretched to break the fall.

Dave writhed swiftly in his bonds and turned on his side to watch his enemy. He saw him crash heavily on to the rocky floor. He waited for the blue man to rise. Jud Whelan never moved.

Hardly able to believe his eyes, Dave watched and waited, but that blue figure remained still where he had fallen.

For one fleeting moment Dave thought, 'He's dead! He must have broken his neck in that fall!'

Then he changed his mind. More likely Jud Whelan had stunned himself. Dave got himself into a sitting position again, the instinct of self-preservation rising high within him. He was very helpless, but while he had a chance, he was going to try to keep his skin intact. But how? How could he, helpless as he was, get away from Whelan before he returned to his senses?

There was only one thing left for Dave and that was to hide. He began to roll, going with the slope so as to make speed. After twenty yards or so, he ran into rocks and that put an end to his rolling. Sweating, he eased himself on to his back and began to shuffle his way in among the rocks, driving himself backwards with his heels.

It wasn't pleasant work. All the time he kept thinking: 'Mebbe I'm just pushing myself on to a nest of rattlesnakes!' That didn't make him feel any more comfortable.

It was slow work, and all the time he could see that long blue snake-like figure lying on the rocks above him. Worse, he knew that Whelan would be able to see him if he came to consciousness.

Suddenly Whelan's arm twitched and moved. The blue man was coming to. Frantically Dave dug his heels into the ground and pressed his wriggling body backwards in an effort to find a hiding place among these rocks. He seemed to move a mere matter of inches each time for all the desperate energy he employed. His body was bathed in perspiration and the bonds around his wrists were almost cutting him in half because they were tightening with the sweat.

He saw Whelan move again. He was rolling over very slowly like a man coming out of sleep and about to sit up. And Dave was still exposed!

Then Dave shoved and found himself falling. That was sickening, too. He felt himself going over the edge of a drop and he didn't know how deep it was beyond. For one wild second he thought 'Gosh, I'm over a precipice!'

And then almost before the thought was completed, he found his shoulders hitting rock again. He had fallen into a shallow rain gully. It was so shallow, in fact, that when he sat up his head came over the level of the wall and he could look across to where Jud Whelan was sitting up shakily, his hand to a face that must have suffered underneath that death mask.

Dave couldn't move any more now without betraying his position. Any sound would bring that crazy ex-miner bounding to his feet after him.

As it was, he watched while the wild figure clambered to his feet, and stood there swaying in the moonlight until he remembered his weapons and went in search of the tomahawk and knife that had flown out of his hands. He found the tomahawk.

Before he had found his knife, Jud Whelan remembered what had happened, and now he began a search for his victim.

It was horrifying to have to sit there and to see that big, crazy man loping around in a systematic search for his bound enemy. Whelan must have known that Dave Oak could not have gone far, and he began to quarter the ground like a hunting dog. It was only a question of time before he found his enemy.

Already he had satisfied himself that the higher part of this hillside did not give cover to Dave Oak. Now he was coming nearer, beginning to search in among the rocks where Dave had taken refuge.

He was within ten yards of Dave, who shrank back to keep his face out of the moonlight.

He could hear Whelan's breath coming in quick gasps under that death mask, and guessed he was still suffering from that fall. Well, that would only make him the more vicious and determined to wipe out the man who knew his secret!

But Dave guessed that he was being relentlessly pursued for another reason, something to do with those silver quarters.

The search came nearer. It was only a question of seconds now before he was discovered. Dave held himself back against the rock wall, out of sight of his enemy now, but listening to the nearing sounds of search.

Then another sound obtruded. It was the clink of bridle metal. At once there was a cessation in those sounds of search behind his head, as if Whelan had heard those clinking noises and had turned his attention towards them.

Dave risked lifting his head. He saw Whelan in silhouette against a silver-grey night sky. Whelan, the crazy would-be medicine man, was standing in a tense attitude staring before him and with no eyes for Dave. Dave switched his eyes to the ground below them.

He saw a horseman slowly riding towards them. When that horse was within a dozen yards of the crouching blue figure, it seemed to halt of its own accord. A crouching man sat like a dark shadow upon that mount.

Dave was horrified. This poor galoot did not know that death crouched above him! At the risk of his own life, Dave gave warning.

Suddenly the night air was rent by his bellow: 'Watch out there! Get your gun goin'!'

That sudden shout brought that weary horse jumping nervously around. The figure on its back seemed to move quickly, accompanying the dancing of the horse.

For one awful moment it seemed as though that snarling, spitting figure perched on the rock just beyond Dave's head would hurl himself in utter ferocity at the helpless Texan. And then the blue-painted figure whirled and darted away towards the shadows. He ran like a man sure that a gun was being raised against him and that a shot would follow any instant.

Desperately, Dave got his feet under him and dragged himself erect. All the time he was shouting to that lone rider. He was warning him of the snake that lurked in the vicinity — was telling that rider to keep his gun up.

The rider never answered him.

The horse was quietening now and

was standing as if rather bewildered below, facing the shouting man.

Dave roared to him to ride across and unfasten him. Any moment he expected to see that lithe blue form came leaping out of the darkness, moonlight glinting upon the flashing blade of his tomahawk. It had happened several times that night. He felt sure it would happen again.

That rider sat there, hunched in his saddle, never moving and never speaking. Quite a minute passed while Dave shouted to that rider, and then his voice trailed away and his eyes stared. It was just about then that he realized he was speaking to a dead man.

When realization did come to him Dave hauled himself over the edge of that shallowy rocky wall and began to edge his way to where that horse was standing. When he was near enough he looked up.

He saw a man wedged between the high pommels of his Mexican type saddle. A man bowed in death with a long Indian war lance sticking through his back.

There was something familiar about that saddle, not usual so far away from the Mexican border. Dave was wondering where he had seen such a horse bearing a Mexican saddle.

Then he realized that it was Hewitt, last of the trio who had ridden from Scalping Knife to win a prize that wasn't theirs.

He looked up at the dead man, silhouetted against the grey night sky, and he thought: 'The poor critter must have ridden into Injuns and got himself killed in a fight!'

Somehow the body had remained in the saddle, while the horse ran wildly wherever it wanted. Or, he checked his thought, perhaps Hewitt had held on to life until a few minutes ago, perhaps even until that shouted warning of his had set the horse prancing.

But one thing he knew even without reaching up to examine Hewitt. At this moment Hewitt was indeed dead.

Dave's eyes abruptly came back to those menacing shadows all around him. Far away in the distance he had heard sounds, and though he couldn't distinguish them at the moment he knew that someone was approaching. He began to roll over that rocky floor, and now he was looking for the knife that had flown from the blue renegade's hand.

It took him minutes to find it, and then it took him more minutes to wedge the knife in a crack in the rocks and set to work to cut through the bonds that fastened his wrists.

And all the time he heard the approach of those horsemen.

They were nearly on to him when he was free. Suddenly his bonds snapped and though the thongs were still gripped tightly into his wrists he could bring his hands before him and grasp that knife and slash through the thongs that bound his feet together. Swaying as the blood circulated back into limbs too long constricted, he picked through the thongs on his wrists with that sharp-pointed knife. Then he was a free man again.

He was free, but Indians were already riding up towards him. He heard a guttural exclamation and guessed that horse and dead rider had been seen.

There was a quickening of those hoofbeats, as if those Indians were racing up to investigate.

He jumped for the horse, and grabbed the guns out of Hewitt's holsters. Hewitt fell from the saddle. That couldn't be helped.

Dave needed that horse, and this was no time for delicacy.

He rammed home those Colts into his own holsters, and then he dragged out a carbine from its scabbard.

Indians were pouring on to that bare moonlit stretch of rock that had been the scene of so much drama in this past hour.

There were dozens of them. This must be another band of defeated

Indians riding westward away from the dreaded rifles of a white man incensed by talk of an Indian massacre.

They saw a solitary paleface climbing up on to a nervous, shying horse, and at once screams rose in their throats — screams of hatred against their traditional enemy.

Dave saw the whites of horses' eyes as they came spurring up to him in an almost solid wall. His gun leapt to his shoulder. He fired, and the echo of that explosion came back in a series of shattering waves from the surrounding tall rocks. An Indian went down. The charge continued.

Dave dragged round his horse and kicked it into speed. For a moment it seemed as though the Indians would be on to him before he could get his horse into its best pace. But then, all at once, the bigger horse got into its stride and began to leave the Indians behind.

Probably those Indians' ponies were exhausted following a pitched battle and then hours of wild flight, whereas Dave's mount was comparatively fresh with having walked these last hours bearing its dead or dying rider.

Exulting, Dave realized that with every stride now he was outdistancing those war-whooping Indians.

He turned in his saddle and shot down one Indian whose pony still seemed to have speed left, and was rapidly coming away from its fellows, even overtaking Dave's fresher horse.

Even so the race wasn't over. A stumble in that moonlight and the pack would be on to him, Dave knew.

He was having to ride at a speed that was reckless in that light, bright though the moonlight was. He plunged his horse across the mesquite, risking gopher holes as he did so. And then, when he climbed even higher into the hills, there was always the danger of sharp rocks reaching up to trip his gallant mount.

He rode in among trees and bushes in a well-wooded high plateau, and there he pulled the oldest trick in the book.

When he had ridden a couple of miles into this cover he plunged his horse towards a thicket of elders that wouldn't betray his entry because the wood was green and soft.

He crashed his horse in among them, flinging himself off as he did so. Then he took a stand by his horse's head, pinching its nostrils so as to prevent it from whinnying when the Indians rode up.

Panting, horse and rider stood there waiting. After an interval the Indians came along, flogging their ponies unmercifully. They rode right past where Dave was standing.

He gave half an hour in order to let the last straggler ride through, then he came out from among those elders and mounted and rode at a right angle to the trail he and the Indians had made until he came to a place suitable for camp.

He dismounted, hobbled his horse,

got Hewitt's blanket and curled up into it as if he were in the safest place in the world.

Before he went to sleep, however, he did some thinking. It was obvious that that blue Indian, who was no Indian, Jud Whelan, was on the trail of those silver quarters himself. Whelan wouldn't know where Ezra Hallet had hidden those missing deeds, and he would be on their trail, wanting to retrieve them for his own crazy purposes. That accounted for his relentless pursuit of the Hallet party, though it puzzled Dave as to why the lean, snake-like ex-miner should take the trail against him, Dave Oak, too.

That was what made Dave think before he allowed himself to drop off into an untroubled sleep. Hadn't Whelan got all four pieces of dollar now? He must have got those from the bodies of the dead Ben Eden and the cowboy sprawled on his face by that tributary of the River Platte.

But did this mean that there was still

one silver quarter that he hadn't got his hands on and which was needed to give him the location of that bag of Federal deeds?

But there was no answer to that problem in the moonlight of that night, so Dave, knowing his plan for the morning, dismissed the subject and went off to sleep.

His plan seemed almost suicidal next day.

If Dave were to help pretty Sue Hallet, as he was determined, then he had to get those silver quarters. To do that he must wrest them from formidable Jud Whelan, the renegade whose hand was against red man and white.

'First, though,' thought Dave ironically, 'I've got to find the varmint.'

He did it by riding to the top of a sheer-walled bluff that rose out of the mesa back almost where he had last encountered Jud Whelan the night before. He rode his horse on to this high point that gave a superb view for miles around, and there he sat and watched and waited.

He knew that if Whelan was in the country he would spot the big Texan sitting there against the blue Wyoming sky upon his horse. But he also knew that every other pair of eyes in the country would see him, and he knew that any such eyes must belong to hostile, warring Indians.

The Indians found him out first. He looked down across the dusty mesquite, and he saw men riding furtively along a deep, shadowy gulch far below him. He grinned to himself. The Shoshones had thought to sneak up on him unawares, but he wasn't to be caught as easily as all that.

As soon as he saw the approaching enemy, Dave pulled round his horse's head, fighting to get it under control as it danced and reared high up on the edge of that bluff. He clapped spurs into its sides and sent it scrambling down the rocky slope that led away from the bluff top.

The Indians never stood a chance against him. He knew all the tricks, and within half an hour was out of sight of any possible pursuer and had so crossed his trail with older hoof marks that he knew they would never be able to track him down.

He rode so as to lead the pursuit away from the bluff, but when he knew he had shaken them off he swung round and calmly rode right back until he was once again sitting his horse on that skyline.

Dave was inviting attack from the blue killer. It was the only way he knew to make contact with Whelan, and he was determined to come back to that high bluff until Whelan came out to do battle with him.

But again Indians came riding up to capture him. No Indian was going to tolerate the sight of a white man in their hunting grounds at that time. The mere sight of a paleface roused their blood fury to boiling point.

Dave growled under his breath when

he saw that second cavalcade of Shoshones sweeping across the mesquite, fanning out to entrap him up on top of that bluff. Again he sent his horse scrambling madly down the north side and went headlong across the mesquite in an effort to shake off the pursuers. This time it was more difficult because these Shoshones were better mounted and had the heels of his horse, tired a little now with carrying Dave's great weight.

But the Texan's superb craft and horsemanship saved him yet again. He got out of sight of his pursuers for just a short while. It was a very short while, but when they saw him again he was streaking off in a totally different direction from the course they had expected him to follow.

By the time they'd turned their ponies' heads after him he had snatched a lead that ensured his safety. The baffled Indians drew rein and shouted their fury and brandished their weapons after the elusive horseman.

Dave turned in his saddle, understanding that faint shout that floated after him, and waved ironically.

An hour later that lone horseman was again slowly climbing the rocky trail that led up on to that bluff. Once again he was riding to tempt danger. Once again he was coming back to that bluff with a view to inviting death.

Only, this time when he reached that bluff, danger and death were already there before him.

7

Besieged!

Dave was ascending the last slopes of that rocky way up to the bluff, when something, perhaps a slight sound, brought his head wheeling round.

He found himself staring at the boulder strewn edge of the bluff to his right. There was a movement among the sprawling rocks. A touch of blue.

Then it was gone. Dave reined at once, and his carbine came leaping into his brown, capable hands. His blue eyes narrowed and he stared at the place where he had last seen his enemy.

Then a movement caught his eye a dozen yards farther along. His gun came leaping round to cover it. He saw that hint of blue, as of a body flashing from one piece of cover to another. It was gone before he could sight, but he knew now beyond a shadow of doubt that his enemy was on top of this bluff before him.

He dismounted then. This way that he had ridden was the only possible way off the bluff. Jud Whelan had placed himself in wait for his enemy, but had put himself into a trap in doing so!

Dave swung out of his creaking saddle, his horse grateful to be relieved of his weight even though it was only for a minute.

Then Dave went slowly, cautiously clambering up the rocky slope to where he had last seen his enemy.

The sweat was pouring from him, running into his eye corners and smarting. But he ignored it. He did not dare divert his attention from the cover so close to hand because of the deadly enemy that lay lurking amidst those rocks.

He manoeuvred until he had got himself on top of a high rock that covered the sloping trail in, and from this point he was able to look down over most of the bluff top.

He saw Jud Whelan then.

Whelan must have known that he was seen and trapped.

Dave saw a movement twenty yards away between a cleft in the rocks that edged the bluff. He saw a hideous, monstrous face. It startled him, and then he realized that he was looking at the death mask of a medicine man — the mask used in times of war or when the dead were being ushered out of the world to join the Great Spirit.

He saw this evil face with its loathsome twining snakes and serpents and scorpions and crawling evil things looking out at him. Dave's gun covered that hideous mask. It didn't move. Dave went walking slowly towards it.

When he was ten yards away he realized that he had been tricked. There was a sound to his left. His head slewed round, though his carbine still covered that mask. Jud Whelan was there, launching himself through the air towards him.

Dave cursed and dropped on one knee and tried to get his gun round. He had fallen for a trick as old as any he had practised that day upon the Indians.

Whelan had left his mask for him to see, and while he had gone across, thinking that Whelan was behind that mask, his enemy had crawled around and taken him unawares upon his flank.

He didn't have time to get his gun up. That blue form with the girdle of human bones came crashing into him even as his carbine lifted. The gun was knocked from his hands, and exploded as the butt danced momentarily on the rocky ground.

Dave went reeling backwards, absorbing the weight of that diving body as he did so. He saw a white face, contorted with fury. He saw blue greased hands reaching for his throat. Then that blue painted form was all over him, hands were digging into his flesh and trying to throttle the life out of him.

It was like fighting with a snarling animal; the ferocity of that attack was unbelievable. It was only later that Dave was to know that Jud Whelan had broken the last of his weapons, his tomahawk, and his attack had been partly designed to dispose of an enemy and partly to secure new weapons for himself.

They rolled madly together, feet and hands going in desperate efforts to subdue the other. And once again, with that small evil head hissing curses so close to his own face, Dave was reminded of a snake. That long, near seven foot length of lean manhood was unnatural in its sinuousness. There was something snake-like about this man who had wanted to become a Snake Indian.

Dave tried to get those hands away from his throat. But Whelan had the reach on him. More, Whelan knew all the tricks of wrestling. He must have been a formidable wrestler in his day.

Dave had to try that old trick that had upset his enemy a few nights earlier. He kept rolling, to shorten that grip on his throat, and each time that Whelan's blue greased body came within reach, he slammed it with all the strength he could.

But his own strength was giving out under that throttling pressure. His eardrums were pounding, and he felt the blood racing in his temples. He knew he couldn't last much longer. He knew that his blows were becoming weaker.

Again he made a desperate attempt to roll himself free. Again that snarling blue body came arching in the air over him. He saw a flat stomach, and he hit with all the strength left in him. It was a last gamble. His fist seemed to go right through that pliant body. Then mercifully the grip on his throat relaxed.

Panting, he raised himself on his elbow. He saw Whelan rolling in agony, his hands clasping his tortured stomach. He passed out of sight behind a rock but not to escape. He reappeared — and now the hideous mask was on his face as he launched himself immediately upon his enemy again. And now, if it were possible, his fury was even greater.

This time Dave hammered away at those reaching hands and kept them from his throat. He staggered to his feet and drove into his enemy with both fists flashing out and hurting. At all costs he must prevent this blue devil from getting his hooked fingers on to him again! Dave felt sure that if once Whelan did secure another handhold, this time the Texan wouldn't be able to fight himself free.

Whelan kept coming in, throwing himself at Dave's legs, trying to trip him, trying to get him down on to the ground where he could secure a stranglehold on the Texan again.

But the big husky manoeuvred lithely, avoiding those ugly rushes and dealing out massive punishment as he did so. He could have used his guns now, those Colts slapping at his belt and hindering him. Yet Dave wouldn't do that. This was a man-to-man fight and he wanted no unfair advantage over his enemy. He was going to lick this blue devil with his naked hands, he thought grimly.

He did, too. There came a moment of utter ferocity, as Whelan recklessly hurled himself at his enemy, his fists pounding and bruising the Texan's face and bringing the blood to his lips and to a cut over his eye.

But Dave fought him off yet again, beat him back until suddenly Whelan had had enough and tried to get away.

Then, even as Whelan turned his long blue legs to leap down the hillside, Dave dived and scooped up his ankles with a mighty swinging right arm. The blue devil went crashing on to his face. By the time he had recovered his senses he found a mighty weight astride his back, his right hand twisted into a lock that was painful and from which he could not release himself.

Dave could only sit for minutes on end, while he recovered his strength. His enemy lay passive, exhausted and recovering his strength, too, and he snatched the mask off and threw it from him.

Then Dave got up and stood back, his hands and clothes filthy with the blue grease that had come from the body of his enemy. He went back, drawing his guns and covering that vicious, reptile-like Jud Whelan. He saw Whelan's head lift, and again he was reminded of an evil striking snake.

Dave said, 'I want them silver quarters, Whelan.' His gun waved imperatively. 'Come on, fellar, give!'

The ex-miner sat up then, and looked his hatred at the cowboy but didn't move.

So Dave walked forward, his eyes blazing. He said, 'I'm gonna get them quarters off you, Whelan. You've got no right to them deeds, and there's people wanting 'em. More than that, I know a gal who's gonna get the reward offered for the recovery of them deeds!'

Still Whelan sat there.

So Dave went right up to him from behind, and slammed his gun barrel into those pliant ribs. He could see a pouch among the bones around the would-be medicine man's girdle. His hand went into it. Whelan's hands dived down in a frantic effort to stop him. Dave pushed that gun even harder into Whelan's back and at once Whelan lifted his hands above his head.

Crazy though he was, Whelan did not want a bullet through his spinal cord. Dave found three silver quarters among some tobacco inside that pouch. He pulled them out. Three quarters.

He said, 'Where's the fourth, Whelan?'

For the first time Dave heard Whelan speak. It was an unpleasant, rather high-pitched, grating voice. Whelan said, 'I don't know. I figgered you might have had it.'

Dave's eyes widened. 'Where's the quarter Tuff Leach had on him? You killed him, didn't you?'

At that the ex-miner didn't answer, and Dave couldn't get him to speak. Jud Whelan wasn't going to help him at all with any information.

After a time Dave recognized it and he retreated towards his horse. He had been watching a dust cloud slowly approaching the bluff far below him, and he knew these would be Indians and once again he would have to ride for his life. He felt sure the big ex-miner didn't know where that fourth quarter was, so there was no use staying with him. He would have liked to have taken Jud Whelan in as prisoner to stand trial for his crimes, but he knew that was impossible. He had to leave him there.

As he got into his saddle he called out to Whelan, 'Your life's a gonner if ever I set eyes on you again. An' we'll be after you with a posse to take you in an' string you up for what you did to Ezra Hallet an' the others!'

That blue figure just stood for a moment and spat at him like an evil beast. Then he saw Jud Whelan go

160

bounding away, those skulls and human bones rattling like a castanet as he did so. He went down that rocky hillside into a coulee and the next thing Dave saw he had come out dragging a horse. The blue apparition mounted and went riding madly away.

Dave set his horse eastwards and rode rapidly away from that advancing dust cloud. His heart was heavy. Three quarters weren't any use to him, he felt certain. Those four adventurers would have taken care that all four quarters were necessary if the secret of the hiding place were to be known.

He rode back across that mesquite, watching all the time for his enemies. For he knew they would be many in that disturbed countryside. Above all he kept watch for Jud Whelan, for he knew the medicine man would never leave him in possession of those three precious quarters.

Dave rode until he was sure he was safe from pursuit. As he was riding he twice saw knots of Indians in the distance heading north, and he felt that he was lucky not to have run into them.

When it was safe he halted and swung down from his weary horse. He found food — dried meat and some corn bread — in a saddle-bag and this he ate ravenously, washing it down with tepid water from a cantina.

That done, he took up a position on a piece of high ground in order to watch while his horse rested and cropped whatever vegetation there was to attract its interest. When he thought it was safe to relax his watch a little he took out those three quarters and put them together, trying to read the message they contained.

It was evident that one man must have buried the treaure — that only one man actually knew the spot.

Dave guessed that man would have been old Ezra Hallet, the kind of man who would be trusted to perform such a task.

Ezra had written one word upon each of these quarters. Dave understood the idea immediately. The three quarters he had each contained a place name. On one was written Black Rock. On another Broken Pine. The third one said Red Cliff.

On the fourth would be some other name or description. It meant that if the man paced out between, say, Black Rock and Broken Pine, and then paced from Red Cliff to that other unknown landmark, where the two lines crossed there the bag of deeds would be found buried.

Dave thought for a while and then decided he knew Black Rock. That was near the scene of the Shoshone war talks of a couple of years back, the place where the Shoshones always met before they went out to war.

Dave sat until he felt that the country was quiet and his horse was rested. Then he rose and went stiffly across to it and swung himself into the Mexican saddle and began to ride slowly northwards.

An hour later Black Rock began to

loom over the horizon.

He approached it cautiously, this huge jutting mass of sombre-looking rocks that reared up from the mesquite.

He dismounted at the foot of this pile called Black Rock, and hid his horse in the high sage and thorn scrub. Then he went on foot to the top of the rock, keeping care to come over the skyline on his stomach in case sharp eyes watched from beyond.

Sharp eyes were beyond! He gasped at what he saw. Ahead of him was a broad basin that gave on to the foothills of the Laramie Range. There were trees here and the country was rougher. He saw where a stream must have meandered across the mesquite, and there he saw along that strip of richer vegetation the unmistakable signs of an Indian camp.

More than that, he could see the Indians and their ponies themselves.

The Shoshones were making more war talk!

Now he understood why those

several parties of Indians were all heading steadily northwards. They had been summoned to the war palaver and were congregating at Black Rock in force. That looked bad for the white people in eastern Wyoming.

He saw the thin plumes of smoke from the camping fires and noticed there were no tepees. That meant there were no womenfolk with them, and that meant a swift foray. He guessed that at any moment they would mount and begin their war ride.

He lingered a few minutes, all the same, wanting to check on this hunch of his that the Black Rock on that silver quarter was indeed this Black Rock of the war talks.

Almost at once he saw a pine tree that had been cleft by lightning, so that its top was over like a broken umbrella, and the whiteness where the weight had torn asunder the trunk was bright in that failing sunshine. That would be Broken Pine.

It was about two or three hundred

yards away from him in the direction of that Indian camp.

His sharp eyes searched round and found Red Cliff. So far it was easy. There was only one red cliff, and that was a scar where a landslide had carried away part of the sloping hill from which that stream appeared to spring. And that was no more than four hundred yards away, but at an angle from that distant broken pine.

Dave looked to his right now, to see what other landmarks might most usefully have been employed by Ezra Hallet. But there were many. Many distinctive trees, and a sharp-edged bluff.

Dave shrugged helplessly. Ezra was too cute a man to be obvious. Dave knew approximately where those precious deeds lay buried, but to find them, a man might dig for thirty years in this ground and still not come upon them.

Suddenly he stiffened. He had caught a new movement from those distant

Indians, and it was significant. Men were out rounding up their ponies.

That meant they were preparing to take the war trail!

Dave looked at the sun. It was descending and would soon be set. It looked as though those Indians proposed to ride all through the night, and if they were going where he thought they were they would come upon their target with first light of dawn.

Tense upon the top of that ugly black mass of rock, Dave watched the Indians run to their ponies. They mounted with quick agile springs, and their shouts came to him quite clearly on the evening air. There was satisfaction in those voices, combined with a savage note that told of their state of mind. This was a war party eager to be on the trail of scalps.

The Indians swung into line behind their chiefs and began to ride eastwards. Dave came down from that rock with little sense of caution. Time was precious now. The dust rose as his heels dug into the sloping hillside as he skidded down as fast as he could. He came off that hillside in long bounding leaps, and went into that high saddle before his horse realized his rider had returned.

It fought discontentedly against a further time on the trail, but lives were at stake and Dave forced its head round and got it travelling at a quick canter.

He rode south a little, and then struck out eastwards. He was hoping to overtake those Indians and pass them on their flank during the darkness.

Night drew on without any sign of those warriors to the north of him. He rode cautiously in the first hours of blackness, increasing his pace as that big moon came up.

But his speed all during the night was depressingly slow. He couldn't help it. His horse had had a hard day and could go no faster now. As it was, by dawn it was foundering fast. It couldn't carry this big man's weight much longer.

With dawn Dave realized that he

hadn't much farther to go. He saw familiar signs ahead of him — that tributary he had first crossed, and in the distance beyond it the frontier town of Scalping Knife.

Resting on top of a hill, he looked behind. There was no sign of pursuit. He removed his old, sweat-stained hat, and let the cool morning breeze dry the perspiration in his hair. He felt satisfied. It seemed that he had got far ahead of pursuit.

Then his satisfaction fled from him. He saw a movement disconcertingly close. A feathered head-dress bobbed into view where a dried-up water-course gave cover half a mile to his right. Behind that head-dress came another war bonnet and behind that yet another.

The Shoshone were right upon his heels! He had gained no more than half a mile's lead during that agonizing night's ride!

Dave realized that he had been seen even as he had seen his enemies. He heard a shout and a brown arm extended and pointed towards him.

He pulled round his horse's head and fanned it with his hat into the nearest it could get to a gallop.

They crossed that stream, Dave allowing his horse to snatch at the water only without pausing. Too much water now, and his beast would go down and never rise again.

Somehow it gained that far bank and climbed it and went staggering towards the distant town that still slept, unaware of the Indian menace closing rapidly upon it.

Dave looked round and saw a mighty throng of Indians come through that water at speed. They weren't much more than a quarter of a mile behind him already.

Desperately he kept that horse going along the rocky trail that led into the town. His eyes searched for signs of life in Scalping Knife, but with the sun only just risen no one as yet had stirred out of doors.

The Indians were on the trail now and catching up. Dave fired his rifle into the air.

His eyes watched that town. There was no answering movement.

Scalping Knife didn't get up simply because someone let rip with a gun. Then Dave's mount went down on its knees, and the way it stayed there told Dave that he had ridden it to the end. That horse couldn't even lift itself now. Dave slid out of the saddle, reloading his carbine.

There was an Indian chief well ahead of his comrades, flat along the neck of a wild mustang. Dave saw the savage delight on that painted face, saw the arm holding the tomahawk lift to make the killing stroke. He felt, almost, the elation which gripped that Indian chief at sight of a lone paleface stranded on the trail.

Dave let him come on.

Then, when that chieftain was no more than fifty yards away and coming in fast, Dave shot him out of the saddle.

He threw away his carbine. As the pony came tearing towards him, mane flying and the whites of its eyes showing, Dave began to run. As the pony came flashing level with him, somehow his hand streaked out and fastened into the mane of that horse and in the same movement he threw himself on to the bare back of that pounding mustang.

His weight nearly threw the beast off its stride and into the rough ground off the trail, but somehow the mustang recovered and went heading straight on towards Scalping Knife.

There was a wild shout of rage from the pursuing Indians, a couple of hundred yards behind him. He took no heed of them. He rode towards Scalping Knife with his six-shooters in his hands, firing them at steady intervals as he came in.

He was a hundred yards from the nearest building — that same building against which poor old Ezra Hallet had collapsed — when he saw the first citizen of Scalping Knife come running into the street. The man was in pants and vest, and nothing else. But he had a gun in his hand.

Dave waved and pointed behind him.

That rifle lifted. Something hummed past Dave's ear as he came riding madly into the town. A bullet went in among the attacking Indians, and brought a pony and rider crashing to the ground. It halted them.

Dave heard the rifleman bawling his head off, shouting a warning to other lay-abed citizens.

Other men were coming running out, all with guns at the ready.

Dave rode into the town shouting, 'Get your guns! Injuns! Everyone out an' make barricades!'

As he rode past that first rifleman he thought he had never seen such an old man in his life. When he saw the others coming out with their guns he thought: 'Goldarn it, only the kids and oldsters have got up!'

Almost at once he understood why.

All the fighting men of the town were still out on the mesquite after the Shoshones.

That was why the Shoshones were attacking this frontier town so boldly. They knew the paleface had been lured deep into the wilderness, and in the absence of the fighting white men they had descended upon this little town to massacre the old and the young, the women and children and the infirm.

Dave saw all that in an instant. Then he saw a kid who couldn't have weighed more than fifty pounds but he looked a tough, wiry youngster. He shouted to him an order.

'Get a hoss, son. Ride like the wind after the men an' tell 'em we need 'em! Tell 'em Scalping Knife's besieged by the Shoshone Injuns!'

8

His Mark!

He saw that boy leap away like mad, proud to have been selected for this rescue ride.

The thin shafts of legs under the ragged jeans fairly twinkled as they took him into a livery stable. The kid didn't ask permission.

The next moment he was riding out on a fine grey.

He'd put a bridle on the horse, but he didn't need a saddle. He was up on that broad back in an instant, and then the hoofs of that grey kicked stones in a rattling fusillade against the clapboard buildings.

Then the boy was off down an alley and on to that wide mesquite just in front of those Indians.

Dave took one look at the kid. He

was satisfied. If any Indians pursued him, they'd never catch that light weight on that fresh horse, their own ponies jaded after a night's march over rough country.

His head slewed round. He saw men everywere running to the edge of the town, rifles gripped ready. But old men and boys, mostly.

The Indians were coming in hell for leather. They were met with a ragged volley of rifle fire that made a lot of noise but didn't do much damage. All the same a few ponies tumbled, and a few riders shouted with the pain of bullet wounds and pulled out from the fight.

The Indians promptly pulled wide and went ringing round that town, their ponies kicking up a slowly ascending dust cloud as they did so. They hadn't expected this.

They had thought to take a sleeping town unawares at the crack of dawn. They had intended to have been rampaging down that main street, killing and looting before the eyes were open of any who remained in Scalping Knife to defend it.

Instead they had run on to wakened men with deadly guns in their hands. Dave had saved the town by a matter of half a minute only!

Men were shouting and he saw forms running through the drifting white powder smoke. Women were about now, scurrying to help their men by bringing ammunition and even spare rifles for them.

They were building barricades at either end of the main street and across the alleys, converting the little frontier town into a crude fortress.

Dave swung off his horse and raced to put his weight behind an old Conestoga wagon that was being pulled towards the west end of the main street. Then it was tipped over on to its side, forming a solid breastwork behind which the defenders could crouch and fight.

The Indians continued their circling

for a few minutes, and then upon a signal all came wheeling in, their cries frightening to listen to.

But those defenders, old or young, had steady hearts and methodically picked off those Indians as they came within range. Again the Indians pulled quickly away from the fight. Indians never did like hand-to-hand fighting. Theirs was a hit and run affair, effective on the plains, but not very fruitful against resolute defenders behind sturdy barricades.

Again they took up their circling, while a group of chieftains pulled out to confer and to plan the next assault. It gave the defenders time to strengthen their barricades and spread their defences more evenly around the perimeter of the town.

Dave found himself going from point to point along the defences, because he was about the only man of his age in that town. He found himself giving orders, telling men how to face the next attack and what to do to make their barricades more secure. He found himself, in fact, taking charge of the defences of Scalping Knife.

He was running across the town, hearing some rifle fire that suggested a sally on the part of the Shoshones, when he saw Sue. She was coming away from where a man sat at ease out on the porch of the Red Eye saloon.

Dave's eyes narrowed, seeing that lone spectator. This was no time for any man to be sitting at ease.

As Sue came running gladly towards him, his eyes continued to look over her head. He saw a man with a thin face that was deep etched with lines that showed a passionate temperament. He had brown eyes that looked bright but with lights that spoke of a sharp and vicious character. He looked young, at any rate not much older than Dave.

Dave's mouth opened to shout an order to that spectator, but then Sue was holding him by the arms and laughing up at him in delight at seeing him safe and sound.

'Oh, Dave,' he heard her exclaim. 'It's wonderful to see you back. I — I thought something might have happened to you.'

He brought his eyes down to look into her lovely blue ones. She looked dainty. Out of place in this rough setting, and yet she was all that a man wanted even on the frontier, Dave was thinking. His smile softened under the sweetness of her glance.

He drawled. 'I sure am glad to see you, too.' Then he lifted his eyes to that man behind her. Almost he had an impression that those bright, sardonic eyes were mocking him. He said, a quick rising anger in him, 'What'n heck's that galoot sittin' up there for? Doesn't he know we're in a fight to death?'

He thought the smile went from Sue's face at that. She didn't answer him directly, but he felt his arm taken quickly and he was wheeled round so that he could no longer look upon the irritating presence of that man outside the Red Eye Saloon.

She was talking, too, and it occurred to him even then that she seemed to be speaking too quickly, as if she was trying to distract him from that stranger.

'I thought you might run into trouble,' she said quickly. 'But you didn't, did you, Dave?'

Dave smiled again. 'Nope.' he said. 'Jes' met up with your three towns-folk — '

'You mean Ed Scholls?'

He nodded. 'Him an' his two pards.' He thought a second and then said with dry humour, 'Nope, I reckon I didn't meet up with much trouble. Jest them three, a blue Injun who wasn't no Injun, an' a pack of Shoshones!' His hand waved to indicate those vengeful, circling warriors out on the mesquite.

She laughed. 'And you call that nothing?'

He grinned.

Then a flight of arrows came sailing into the town, while simultaneously there was an angry volley of rifle fire, as if the defenders had opened up upon incautious Indians racing in to discharge their more primitive weapons.

Dave saw the first arrow smack into warped wood-work, shattering as it did so. He grabbed Sue and dragged her under the steps by a dry goods store. They saw the other arrows break on the road and buildings around them, and no one got hurt. When the shooting died, they came out.

Dave said: 'They're maybe only arrows, but I don't take chances. Arrows can kill — that's why the Injun uses 'em!'

He found the girl smiling up at him, and only then did he realize he was holding her hand. She said: 'I wouldn't want anything to happen to you, Dave!'

He found his heart bumping a little faster. 'No?'

'No.' She was a mere slip of a girl, but decisive. She was frank, too, in the way of those frontierswomen. She said, just a little wistfully: 'I think you're all

I've got in the way of friends, Dave!'

It made Dave stiffen a little to hear it, and he looked down at her in something like bewilderment. He had only known her a few hours, and yet he was being told he was the only friend she had.

'I only just came here,' she explained. 'I don't know many people. Of course, Dad had friends.'

Dave said: 'Sure, your Dad had friends.' And then he said, his words coming all of a rush: 'I sure am mighty proud to think I'm your best friend, Sue. You'll find me all you want in the way of friends.'

He couldn't stand to speak with her after that. A hot wave of embarrassment seemed to rise up within him, and he had to turn suddenly and plunge away towards the barricades.

If he had turned he would have seen pretty Sue Hallet looking after him, a smile upon her lips that was tender and proud. Sue knew instinctively that here was a man worth having, and she knew

183

he was hers for the asking.

Dave didn't know what thoughts were going through that shrewd little mind of Sue Hallet. He couldn't believe his good fortune — that he had met such a wonderful girl and that she should value his friendship so highly.

He came back to those barricades with his brain in a whirl, but what he saw drove away all thought of Sue Hallet right then. The Indians had been conferring out in a solid mass on the mesquite to the west of the town. They were clearly being harangued by someone in their midst, and time after time deep-throated roars of savage approval floated across to the ears of the crouching defenders.

But just as Dave rode up, that compact force fanned out into a wide line that immediately began a thunderous charge upon the defences.

It was frightening, terrifying, that massed line of attackers. But what brought Dave's eyes wide open and an exclamation to his throat was sight of the man who rode in the lead of those Shoshones.

He was a man who rode a pony so small that it served only to accentuate his great length. He was a man who screamed like an Indian, but was no Indian.

He was a man who was painted blue from head to foot, save for his face which was the face of — Jud Whelan, the renegade ex-miner!

Dave shouted for reserve defenders to come running up to this point to meet the attack. They came as fast as they could, but some were stiff-limbed, old men whose fighting days were long over.

Dave's heart sank as he saw the defenders who had to match up and defeat these savage Indian warriors.

He was thinking: 'They can't hold on. If these Injuns just keep a-comin', they can ride right through our defences and capture the town within five minutes.'

His eyes lifted towards the west, in

the direction that kid had taken, riding to bring the fighting men back to Scalping Knife. There was no sign of him on that horizon. It would probably be hours before he began to return. Meanwhile, they had to hold on until relief came to them.

Guns roared, and Indians rolled into the dust. The charge came on. Dave sighted for the blue figure that clearly was leading these Indians on in their mad charge. He fired. He must have missed because the blue figure still came on with screaming hatred on his lips.

The defenders fired another volley and more ponies and riders went down. But still those Indians charged on. Frantically Dave sighted again and fired, but again some sudden, unpredicted movement of that horse saved the life of its rider. Jud Whelan still came on!

Again the defenders got their rifles sighted and simultaneously fired a third volley. This time those Indians were no more than forty yards away and coming in fast. It was slaughter. At that range not a gun could possibly miss.

Ponies went down, kicking and screaming in their pain. Riders came crashing to the dusty mesquite, and those who could immediately began to crawl away — there were others who lay painfully still.

It was too much for the Indians, undisciplined to this type of warfare. In spite of that savage white leader of theirs they turned and fled out of range of the white man's deadly rifles.

Sweating from the excitement of that moment, Dave could only think: 'If they'd kept on for another ten seconds they'd have been in among us and the fight would have been over!'

Dave and those other defenders watched the Indians ride out of range, and a few still had the heart to raise a cheer at the discomfiture of those warriors.

'I reckon we've got 'em licked!' bragged one toothless old-timer who should have known better. But there were others who just looked at him and then looked at that mighty war array circling sullenly out on the mesquite and they couldn't share his delight.

Another settler spat brown tobacco juice into the dust and said soberly: 'They don't always stop. There'll come a time when they'll keep on ridin' an' then we won't be able to keep 'em out!'

The speaker spat again and then his eyes glared venomously at that blue figure trailing after the defeated warriors. 'By glory. I'd like to get my hands on that varmin!' he cursed.

These men had recognized the renegade, and now their hearts were full of hatred towards the ex-miner. The fact that he was a bit crazy didn't soften their judgment at all. White men shouldn't fight with Indians against white men, was their code.

Dave leaned on the hot barrel of his rifle and stared out after that wild blue figure on that small Indian pony. Plainly Whelan was furious with those Indians and was cursing them roundly for losing heart just when they did.

Without hearing a word, Dave guessed what he was saying. He'd be telling them they should have gone on. That they'd pulled out of the fight right at the moment when victory was in their grasp.

The settlers could see the sullen Indians facing that solitary white man. Some of them wondered why it was the Shoshones had been prepared to accept him into their midst — him a hated white man at that.

'I reckon they know him to be a valuable ally,' one defender muttered in explanation. It didn't matter under what terms he rode with the Indians. In the end it amounted to the same thing — he was leading the red enemy against them.

Dave felt someone come and stand close to him. Then he heard a harsh voice say: 'Now, what do you suppose that galoot's got in mind — that he'll attack a town openly?'

Dave turned. That *hombre* who had been sitting on the Red Eye porch was standing by his side, a queer mocking, calculating grin on his face. Again Dave had the impression that the fellow was laughing at him — no, jeering, that was the word.

Before Dave had time to say anything, the fellow went on: 'Looks mighty like there's somethin' in this town he's after. Looks like he'll kill every man-jack in Scalpin 'Knife in order to get what he wants, too!'

Again that long-faced, mean-eyed *hombre* jeered at Dave, and he said once more: 'I wonder what it is he wants?'

Saying which, though without waiting for an answer, the *hombre* turned and walked away. This time, though, he walked towards a barricade, and his long-barrelled Navy Colt was out. Evidently he had changed his mind. Evidently he intended to help in the defence of the town. Dave couldn't say anything to him now on that score, although he felt irritated and wanted to brass off the jeering-voiced stranger.

He might have done something about it, too, only at that moment some of the women came down with food and drink for their menfolk. Sue was among them. She came up to Dave, smiling her prettiest for him. There was coffee in a big can and a plate of meat and bread. Several men stood around and shared the food and drink, Dave among them.

But he didn't share Sue. They stood apart and talked in soft tones to each other.

Dave looked towards the *hombre* and said: 'There's a fellar there kinda askin' fer trouble!' Sue's hand flew to grip his arm as if in sudden anxiety. 'He kinda gets in my hair!' said Dave nastily.

'Don't cross that man,' Sue whispered anxiously. 'He's a mean man, Dave, and — and I'm afraid of him!'

Dave's eyes switched quickly towards hers. 'Afraid?' he queried. He didn't understand such an expression from the girl. But she didn't explain.

So Dave went on. 'He seems like he knows more than he lets on. He seems to know somethin' about that blue devil yonder.' His nod went towards where Jud Whelan was haranguing these sullen Indians again. By the sound of it he was meeting with success, too, for with increasing frequency those Indians came back with savage growls of approval.

'There's something I haven't told you,' Dave said to Sue. 'Guess I just haven't had time to talk to you about my trip after them silver quarters.'

Sue just shrugged a little and turned away disinterestedly. That again puzzled the big Texan.

'Don't you want to hear about them?' he asked.

Sue turned and smiled at him and spoke quickly, too quickly. 'Oh, yes. Do tell me, Dave. Did you — find them?'

Yet again Dave had the impression that Sue was holding something in reserve for him, that she was forcing this interest in those silver quarters. It was too puzzling for him to understand at all. He thought he must surely be mistaken.

He told her. 'I got three of 'em. I reckon I was mighty lucky to get those three, too. But there's still a fourth — without it these three aren't any good. Now,' he said thoughtfully, 'I wonder where I can get that fourth quarter from?'

When all this fighting was over he would have to go out and look for the fourth member of the Hallet expedition, and see if he could find that missing silver quarter.

Then he thought, 'Mebbe there isn't goin' to be an end to this fightin' for me.'

Again those Indians were spreading out, and Dave knew they would be more dangerous this time because they had learned from their first wild charges. It wouldn't be long before some of the Indians crashed in among the defences, and then it would be all up with them.

Dave's eyes went quickly again towards the western horizon. If only that kid could find the menfolk pretty soon and bring them back to their rescue, he thought. He looked towards those massed Indians, and decided that help would have to come mighty soon.

Then he realized that the Indians had changed their tactics. Perhaps in spite of the threats and cajolings of the renegade, they hadn't the heart to make another frontal attack. Instead they had compromised with new tactics which seemed less expensive on life than charging barricades.

It took the defenders some minutes before they realized the purpose of this new manoeuvre. The Indians split up into two parties, one containing no more than a couple of dozen mounted braves, with the rest of the Shoshones numbering at least two hundred, farther to the north of them.

The settlers kept their eyes upon the larger force.

Suddenly it seemed as if an attack

was about to be mounted. Those Indians in the main party began to shout their war cry and surged forward. Every eye watched them, every gun was trained to meet this threatened charge.

While the defenders were occupied watching the main Shoshone force, the smaller group of picked warriors suddenly came charging in towards the town.

When they were still fifty or sixty yards out they let fire with arrows which had been held on the blind side of their horses.

Dave caught a hint of smoke curling through the air as those arrows sailed gracefully towards the wooden buildings. He understood at once.

'Fire bugs,' he yelled. 'The Injun is goin' to set fire to Scalpin' Knife!' He roared to the defenders to keep their positions at the barricades, and then he went racing off towards the centre of the town opposite which the Indians had discharged their bows. Now they were riding rapidly away, while some of their arrows began to burn furiously on the roofs of the sun-dried clapboard buildings.

Dave roared to the defenders nearest the flames to put them out. He himself scrambled frantically up on top of the porch of a gaming establishment, and began to beat out the spreading flames with his hat. A pail of water was handed up to him by one of the women and he threw it on to the fire. It hissed for a second and then went out.

By this time another arrow a few yards away from him had established a much bigger fire. Half a roof was beginning to burn gaily. The slight wind from the mesquite fanned the flames rapidly through the tinder dry, bleached boards.

Beating at these flames with his hat did no good, and then, when the water came, this time it was slow in arriving and was too late.

Dave threw it on to the flames, but it had no apparent effect. It was too hot up there to remain now, and with the building roaring into a mighty pyre of smoke and flame, Dave was forced to retreat. He dropped into the street.

Sue was standing there watching anxiously, waiting for him. He heard her say, 'We'll never put those flames out. They're burning the town over our heads.'

Dave said grimly, 'You're dead right, Sue. We can't stop this now.'

Then his eyes glanced out to where that thin blue figure was sitting in malevolent triumph on that Indian pony out on the mesquite.

'I'll bet that darned renegade is mighty pleased with himself right now,' Dave told the girl. His eyes smouldered with rage. If he could have had hold of the renegade at that moment it would have fared ill with the man.

The heat of those spreading flames drove them back towards the western barricade. The town, all in the space of five minutes, was a sea of jumping flames. There wasn't going to be any part of the town left when this battle was over, everyone knew.

What worried them, though, was that the heat of these flames looked as though they would drive the defenders out on to the open mesquite.

Dave thought, 'We won't stand any chance there.'

The Indians would be able to ride in among them, unprotected by barricades and defences this time. They would be over-run and cut down in a matter of seconds.

At the thought his arm went round the girl and held her tightly to him. That was a fate he didn't dare contemplate for lovely Sue Hallet.

Suddenly he determined it wasn't going to happen to her. At all costs he was going to hold the defenders together until relief came. He was pretty sure that kid would meet the young men of the town returning to Scalpin' Knife. They wouldn't be long in coming in, he felt certain, but all the same it was vitally important that he played for time.

When the heat was so great that the paintwork was blistering on those tables and chests that were piled up as emergency barricades at the street end, Dave gave the order to pull aside that barricade and for all the townspeople to retreat out on to the open mesquite.

There was a mighty roar from the waiting Indians at that. Their trick had succeeded! The people of Scalpin' Knife had been forced out into the open by those fires they had started. Now they were at their mercy and could be overrun and hacked out of existence.

Dave didn't let himself think of that just then. He told the defenders to march out a hundred yards into the desert and then to dig themselves in as best they could with their hands. He himself went out with them, his arm around Sue's slim shoulders.

She raised no objection. She knew it was right for him to be looking after her in this emergency.

They went to ground among some

mesquite bushes just as those Indians fanned into a huge semi-circle preparatory to making that final charge. In their midst was that wild blue figure whose crazy genius had brought the settlers to this near moment of defeat. Dave lay in the dust, cuddling his rifle and watching those Indians. Some horses strayed across his line of vision. They had been turned loose from their stables in the town when the place went up in flames. Now they trotted aimlessly about, not understanding their unusual freedom.

Dave realized that someone was lying close to him. When he turned he found himself looking into that long, sallow, lined face of the man who'd thought to be a spectator of the fight.

Dave said sourly, 'You had to take part in this scrap after all, didn't you?'

The man's eyes shifted. He was trying to think of something unpleasant to say. At last it came out. 'I reckon you won't feel so chippity for long, big fellar. That danged blue Injun's got his mark on you!'

He paused and then said significantly, 'Reckon you'd better give me them three quarter dollars right now afore he puts a tomahawk in your thick skull.'

And then he added another sentence that was mystifying to the Texan. 'They're mine, anyway.'

9

Showdown

Dave hadn't time to express his wonder. There was movement among those Indians now as if they were coming back into the charge. He saw the skirmishing, and recognized that fierce voice of the renegade exhorting them to wipe out the white men this time. That was the sort of talk these savage Shoshones would listen to.

Then Dave felt a tug at his arm. It was Sue. He turned, blinking against the light as he faced up towards the sun.

Sue wasn't looking at him, however. There was a look of strained excitement on her pretty face, and her eyes were turned towards the western horizon.

He heard her say, swiftly, softly,

'Dave, what does that look like?'

He knelt up beside her. She was pointing far across the mesquite. He saw a tiny cloud of dust many miles away.

His eyes narrowed. 'Could be they're riders,' he said.

Sue clutched his arm. 'They're the men,' she said quickly, eagerly. 'They're our men, Dave. Oh, if only we can hold out long enough, we'll be saved!'

Dave said slowly, 'Yeah, mebbe they are our men. But could be they're Injuns, Sue! Reinforcements for these critters!'

Yet in his heart he knew she was right.

He knew these were the returning fighting men of Scalping Knife.

His eyes switched towards those massed Indians. At any moment they would come plunging towards this little party, alone there on the dusty mesquite with the smoke of the town swirling around them.

There was one thought hammering

now in Dave's mind. If these Indians charged, that would be the end of this party. They were without protection now, and that horde of Indians would be in among them within seconds. These men were too old to be of any use in hand-to-hand fighting — and the boys were too young and without the strength to grapple with fierce warriors at close quarters.

It would be the end.

But a thought was hammering in his brain: If only these Indians can be delayed in their charge for another ten minutes or so then the citizens of Scalping Knife might be saved by their advancing comrades.

An idea leapt into his mind. Sue was startled to feel him rear to his feet, and then go plunging away out of her grasp. She called, 'What's the matter, Dave?' And then concern leapt into her mind as she called again, 'What are you going to do?'

But Dave didn't even hear her. His mind was set on his mission ahead. He was going to stop that Indian charge single-handed!

He ran towards a horse. It wasn't the horse he had ridden into the town. This was a fine glossy black, and it trailed a head rope. Dave ran alongside of it and leapt nimbly on to its back as, too late, it decided to prance away.

He grabbed that head rope, and pulled the horse round to face towards the Shoshone Indians.

That action of his had attracted their attention, and all eyes were upon him. He saw that Whelan the renegade was right out in front of the line now, as if taking up a position to lead them in that last mad charge.

Dave kicked his heels into those smooth black sides of that mighty horse. It bounded forward. Bounded towards those Shoshone Indians and the wild blue crazy figure that stood out in the lead.

As Dave rode towards the enemy there was a scream of horror from behind him. That was Sue, in anguish now to see what he was doing. There was a murmur of astonishment and dismay from the other people huddled down into the sandy waste.

But Dave rode grimly on towards that mighty enemy.

For some reason it made Jud Whelan kick his heels into his horse's sides and ride out towards Dave. That was just what Dave was wanting.

The two horsemen rode together while Indians and whites looked on wonderingly.

When they were still fifty yards apart Dave shouted, 'Jud Whelan, I'm comin' to get you!'

He saw Whelan's small head above that blue-streaked torso snarl hatred at him. He saw Whelan brandish his tomahawk and upon an impulse Dave swung down from his great black and picked up a tomahawk that lay fallen in the mesquite.

Whelan had halted, not understanding that manoeuvre.

Dave came walking his mount

towards the renegade.

He shouted again, loud enough for the Indians to hear, 'There's only one thing to be done to a renegade, Whelan. I'm gonna do it to you!'

He could have done it with his guns, swiftly and without danger to himself, because Whelan wasn't armed with anything except the weapons of these Indians.

But Dave didn't want to put an end to the renegade quickly. He wanted to use the life of this renegade to save the lives of these helpless people out on the mesquite. He wanted this to be a long combat, lasting until relief came riding up. It meant risking his own life all that time, but he was prepared to take that risk in order to help his kind.

Jud Whelan lifted his long thin body high and brandished his tomahawk ferociously. Then he started to charge upon the Texan, confident he could use that tomahawk better than big Dave Oak.

That stopped the charge of those

Indians. They realized that here was something personal, that this was to be a fight to the death, and they were eager to watch it. Their eyes were absorbed by those two charging figures, and forgotten for the moment was their own desire to ride in among the white people and kill them. Their brown eyes saw the two figures crash together.

They rode right into each other. Neither would pull out from that charge. Their horses ran shoulder to shoulder, and their riders leaned forward and swung savagely at each other with those gleaming tomahawks.

Dave thought he'd hit, but somehow the elusive blue figure drew to one side at the last second and he cut only air. The snarl upon Whelan's face turned to triumph as his own blade came descending towards Dave's shoulder. He rode under it and took the blow across his collar bone, only it was the shaft that hit him and not the blade.

Both riders pulled out and circled again for another charge. Dave looked westwards quickly. That dust cloud seemed no bigger.

Sweating, he pulled his nervous, skittish horse round and set it towards the renegade again.

This time the horses did some side-stepping at the last moment to avoid each other, and the momentum of the charge was lost. The two combatants found themselves side by side, facing each other. Each grabbed for the other's tomahawk, so that they sat their mounts, locked in each other's embrace, neither capable of moving for a minute.

Then the horses pulled apart and both riders had to let go. As they did so, each savagely whirled his blade and tried to get in a blow. Both missed.

Again that circling movement to come round on each other in another fierce charge. Breathlessly everyone watched that silent, deadly combat.

Dave's calculating eyes looked again towards that dust cloud. It was awfully, awfully far away!

He sighed. He had to keep on wasting time until help came to them. Grimly setting his teeth, he plunged back into the fray.

Again those horses wouldn't crash into each other. That first time had hurt and they had learnt their lesson. Again they pulled aside when they were almost on top of each other, rearing and whinnying as they lifted their proud heads into the blue Wyoming sky.

When they came down on all fours the riders leaned across and cut ferociously at each other.

This time both hit.

Dave thought his arm had been chopped off — his right arm, the one bearing the tomahawk.

Whelan's blade caught him on the bicep, and though it was more a bruising blow than a cut because at the last moment he managed to pull away from the descending weapon, yet it crippled that arm and left it useless for the remainder of that fight.

Dave shifted the tomahawk to his left

hand. There was blood on it. He, too, had caught Whelan in the arm.

He could see blood mingling with the blue on the renegade's arm just above the wrist. But it couldn't have been such a crippling blow, because Whelan hadn't taken his tomahawk in his left hand.

Dave pulled out of the fight then. That was good tactics, anyway, because it prolonged this fight and gave the Scalping Knife men chance to ride up.

He could hardly see that distant dust cloud because of the sweat that rolled from his eyebrows into the corners of his eyes.

He pulled round and though he heard another cry of terror from Sue, out there on the mesquite, he set his horse plunging back towards Whelan.

This time, as they came near, Dave skilfully kneed his mount so as to come unexpectedly on Whelan's left side. That meant that Whelan had to swing across his own body in order to hit out at him, and that shortened its reach.

It was the only way Dave could compensate for a left arm which was not as effective as his right.

The two tomahawks crashed together this time, and then were held by interlocking blades. The two riders struggled to pull the other off his mount. Both were too secure.

Suddenly, desperately, Dave released his tomahawk and grabbed for the wrist of that renegade. It was a quick move and might have been effective, but for the grease on that thin, wiry arm. Dave tried to heave Whelan right off his horse, and he might have succeeded if only his hand had been able to retain a grip.

As it was, the wrist slid through Dave's grasping fingers. He plucked the tomahawk out of Whelan's hand all the same, and tried a quick back-hand blow that was partly effective. The side of the blade crashed into Whelan's ribs and he pulled out of the fight with a loud gasping noise that showed he was in pain.

Whelan was down off his horse like a flash, picking up Dave's tomahawk. Then the two were back at each other, fighting like bantam cocks.

The dust rose about them, sometimes hiding them from view of the breathless spectators, white and red. Dave was handicapped by his injured arm, but he rode in under Whelan's vicious, sweeping tomahawk, and now had the renegade gripped around his greasy blue waist. Somehow he managed to catch hold of that tomahawk with a right arm that was almost useless, and for the moment the contestants sat there on their horses, glaring at each other and powerless to move.

Dave looked at that fury-contorted face upon that long thin body. He snarled at the blue-painted ex-miner, 'You renegade! You're goin' to get your chips for leadin' Injuns agen your own kind!'

Whelan snarled back, 'I ain't no white man any more. Not after the way I was treated.'

Whelan's eyes blazed in an almost maniacal fury.

'That darned surveyor cheated me out of my lands! OK, if I can't have any mining land, so help me, no one else is going to have any!'

Dave managed to grin, straining to hold that writhing form. He said: 'They'll have their mines. We'll get those deeds. I'm gonna get that fourth quarter, somehow, somewhere!'

Whelan knew what Dave was talking about. He snarled, 'You're wrong, pardner. I'm gonna kill you an' get them quarters for myself!'

They heaved simultaneously, and rocked and almost came off their horses. Then one of the horses shied and pulled quickly away and both men fell to the ground locked in embrace. Dave twisted and managed to fall on top of his opponent. It hurt, and he heard Whelan yelp out. Dave got to his feet. Whelan came bounding up. Dave was in like lightning, his left arm swinging.

He got Whelan a mighty blow on the chest that sent the taller man staggering back on to the mesquite.

Dave wiped the sweat out of his eyes. He risked a quick glance behind him. His heart jumped. That cloud of dust had swelled to large proportions. They were nearer now, those fighting men of Scalping Knife.

He turned back towards his opponent, thinking, 'I've only got to hang on another minute or so now!'

He glanced at the Indians. They were watching him — all except one Indian, although Dave wasn't to know that.

Dave could have used his Colts now upon Whelan, but still he wanted to play for time and Colts did things quickly.

Whelan came bounding in again, brandishing his tomahawk. Dave had lost his and was without suitable means of defence.

Crouched, his knees bent a little, Dave leapt to one side as Whelan charged by. A roar went up from the spectators at the speed of this manoeuvre, and at the stunning blow that Dave gave to Whelan as he passed. The renegade crashed to the dust, snarling and spitting. But in a second he was on his feet again.

Dave almost felt despair in his heart. He began to think this ex-miner would always come charging at him with that brandishing tomahawk — would keep on no matter how much punishment he took, until he got in that one blow with his keen-edged blade that would put an end to Dave altogether.

But he had to risk it, Dave kept telling himself. Even though his own life was lost, he had to hold the attention of those Indians another few minutes longer.

He failed.

An Indian was pointing, his long brown arm outstretched rigidly. Dave heard a wild cry that ran down the line of Indians at that.

He looked up. All the eyes of those Indians were now turned to watch that approaching dust cloud.

Dave groaned. Almost, he thought, he had succeeded. But not quite. That dust cloud was still some distance away.

He saw the Indians kick their horses into motion. They weren't going to be cheated of vengeance now. Now they would ride down upon that little group of people and slay them before their fellows arrived.

He heard the cries from those Indian throats as they came in a mad charge towards their prey. And Dave realized that he was right in the middle of the battle.

Whelan flung his blue-painted form at his enemy again, just then. Dave found that irrespective of the events around him, he had to fight for his life with this crazy ex-miner.

This time Whelan got in and grappled with the wounded Texan.

Dave couldn't get in one of those powerful blows that would settle most men and even discomfited the ex-miner.

The Indians were almost on top of them. Dave saw fierce, war-painted faces glaring at him as they charged up. He saw the sticking lances poised ready for a thrust as they rode by.

He knew they would never pass him and leave him alive. He was their target.

The Indian ponies were almost on top of him. He saw those nearest Indians lift in their saddles, their arms held rigidly high over their heads, gripping those lances.

Then Whelan, oblivious to what was happening around him, kicked behind Dave's braced legs and both toppled to the ground.

There was a thunder of hoofs all around them. Dust rose and billowed over the two fighting men.

And Dave was lying on his good left arm now.

His right arm was too weak to hold

back that blow. Whelan was in triumph, rolling on top of him, that tomahawk poised, about to dash the life out of his hated enemy.

Then Whelan sagged. The tomahawk dropped from his grip. He collapsed on top of Dave.

The thunder was passed in a second. The dust began to settle. Dave threw off that weight upon him.

He staggered to his feet. Three lances protruded from the back of that renegade. Whelan had saved Dave's life in that moment when he had reared on top of the Texan to dash his life out.

Dave began to run after the Indians. Both Colts were out now. There was gunfire. It was savage, and must have been intimidating to the Indians even then. But they were riding on, riding straight towards the crouching defenders in the desert.

Dave saw forms materialize out of that dust cloud just beyond the defenders on the mesquite. His heart leapt. The fighting men of Scalping

Knife were closer than he had thought! They would arrive at the scene of battle simultaneously with the Indians!

It was their guns, added to those of their fellows, that were putting such a murderous hail of lead in among those charging Indians.

Dave kept on running until he found a stray Indian pony, which he caught and mounted.

The battle was raging. The newcomers from the west had charged their horses in among the Shoshones. Guns were roaring off, and rifles were being used as clubs.

Dave came streaking in behind those Indians, his Colts leaping as he triggered lead.

Then he was in among them, a Colt reversed in his left hand, clubbing Indians out of his way as he fought to get through to his kind.

He got through. There was no one able to stop that mighty Texan in his present warlike mood.

He got through and circled his horse

before where he saw Sue crouching. No Indian was going to get through to take her!

Then the Indians threw in the sponge. Suddenly they'd had enough of fighting these white men with their terrible weapons.

They began to go out of the fight. Suddenly that fight was a rout, with Indians streaming northwards across the mesquite and some of the Scalping Knife young men ran after them.

The battle had been won. Their town was burnt out, but at least the lives of their people had been saved.

★   ★   ★

It was dark. Camping out on the mesquite alongside the burnt-out ruins of Scalping Knife was no hardship in the warmth of that summer's night.

There were camp-fires, and enough wood and canvas had been salvaged to make huts to accommodate the wounded, the womenfolk and children.

Now the weary frontiers-people were resting after their supper. The talk around the campfires was becoming desultory and sleepy.

Dave saw Sue and walked across to her. They hadn't had much chance to talk since he came back.

The Texan said, 'Things are goin' to be all right, Sue.' She flashed a smile up at him. 'It doesn't take long for pioneering folk to build another town.'

She smiled. 'You talk as if you think I'm going to stay out here at Scalping Knife.'

Dave watched her carefully. 'Could be,' he said. 'Mebbe you wouldn't do so badly at that if you did stay.'

Her eyes dropped. 'It's no place for a single girl,' she murmured.

Dave took hold of her hand. Earnestly he said, 'Look, Sue, I don't want you to be single. This is a place where a man can buy land and rear cattle and hosses and grow good crops. All a man needs is money.'

Sue whispered, 'But we haven't

222

money, Dave. Neither you nor I have enough to start ranching.'

It was her answer, all the same. Dave's heart exulted. Now he felt he could do anything. Sue was his!

Words poured from him. 'There's that ten-thousand dollars, Sue. All I've got to do is find that extra silver quarter and the reward's yours. It'll be easy enough to find the exact spot where them deeds was hidden.'

Then he realized that Sue was troubled. Her eyes lifted to his unhappily. There was pity on her lovely face.

'Dave, you don't know,' she whispered, and there was agony in her voice. 'We can never get that reward now.'

Dave was stunned. He said, 'I don't know what you mean. It's rightly yours.'

She shook her head. 'No, Dave,' she said. 'I'm afraid — '

A voice broke in upon them then. It was an ugly, jeering voice. Someone had been listening.

'Nope. I reckon them quarters is rightly mine!'

Dave turned. There was a man standing with a silver quarter in his hand. But the other hand was outstretched, inviting the three that Dave held.

Dave lifted his eyes. He saw that long, sallow face with the deep lines in it that denoted fierce passion. The man was triumphant.

Sue whispered, 'This is Tuff Leech. I was trying to tell you, Dave!'

Leech grinned. 'It was mighty good of you to collect them silver quarters for me, Texan. They're mine. I'm the sole survivor and that's how it was fixed. The one to come through took the pool. I came through. I got away from that blue devil yonder!'

Dave said slowly, 'Not so fast.' His brain was racing. He was remembering suspicions.

He said slowly, 'There was one of your pards didn't die from an Indian weapon.' He knew he was on to something immediately. He saw Tuff Leech flinch and his face go a little white. Dave pressed home his advantage.

'Yeah,' he said slowly. 'There was a poor old man who was shot with a gun. And that's not an Injun weapon around these parts.'

Leech licked his lips and then started to bluff. 'It was an accident,' he said quickly, saying more than he should have done. 'I don't know how you know, but I couldn't help it. I was cleaning my gun.'

Dave shook his head. He'd heard of men cleaning their guns before.

The big husky's voice grew hard. 'It was queer about that bullet wound,' he rapped. His eyes didn't leave that thin, sallow face now. It was no longer confident and sardonic.

Leech licked his lips. Men were crowding round, watching — guessing. Leech's eyes shot quickly from one hard face to another. 'I don't know what you mean,' he almost whispered. His hand was going slowly towards his gun.

Dave told him. 'That bullet went into old Ben's back,' he snapped, and at that the crowd came surging forward, eyes blazing.

Leech cracked then. He had been so confident of having covered himself over that crime — the sole witnesses were dead, obligingly killed by that crazy, would-be Indian, ex-miner Whelan. No one would ever know what he had done, he had been telling himself.

And now this big, brown-faced Texan had stumbled on the truth.

It was too much. Leech lost his head and went for his gun. Anyway, he thought he had the drop on the big fellow. Leech's hand was almost on his gun butt before the Texan saw the move.

There was a wild scurry of confusion as men hurled themselves out of the line of fire. Dave shoved out and pushed bonny Sue Hallet behind him. Then he went reeling sideways, his hands stabbing holsterwards.

His guns came out talking, belching flame.

Leech screamed, his guns flaming, too. Lead had ripped into his shoulder muscles. He went reeling, staggering, sobbing in pain. A bully who couldn't take the medicine he had so often dealt to others. Men came forward, saying, 'That was quick shootin', pardner. You'd have got him proper if you'd had time to get your gun straight afore triggerin'.'

But Sue knew different, Sue clambering shakily to her feet.

She knew that Dave Oak had hit where he wanted to hit, had fired to disarm and not to kill. That was the kind of man Dave Oak was, and her heart swelled to think of it.

She went over to him, smiling, as the crowd took Leech away — a prisoner who would stand fair trial and then suffer whatever justice decreed.

She stroked the mighty arm of that Texan, whispering, 'Everything's all right now, Dave.'

'Everythin',' he smiled back. 'Leech an' Whelan aren't to be feared now. Nor them Injuns.'

He put his arm round her and walked her into the dusk. He was thinking he'd retrieve that fourth quarter when they'd finished with Leech; he'd go and get those deeds and claim the reward for Sue.

And then — He looked into the darkness. This was good country. He'd set to breeding horses. With Sue that would be a life worth living.

A ranch of his own after all these years rolling around! And the loveliest girl in the state, he thought jubilantly, and his grip tightened about her shoulders. She turned her smiling, lovely face towards his . . .

THE END

We do hope that you have enjoyed reading this large print book.

Did you know that all of our titles are available for purchase?

We publish a wide range of high quality large print books including:
Romances, Mysteries, Classics
General Fiction
Non Fiction and Westerns

Special interest titles available in large print are:
The Little Oxford Dictionary
Music Book, Song Book
Hymn Book, Service Book

Also available from us courtesy of Oxford University Press:
Young Readers' Dictionary
(large print edition)
Young Readers' Thesaurus
(large print edition)

For further information or a free brochure, please contact us at:
Ulverscroft Large Print Books Ltd.,
The Green, Bradgate Road, Anstey,
Leicester, LE7 7FU, England.
Tel: (00 44) **0116 236 4325**
Fax: (00 44) **0116 234 0205**

Other titles in the
Linford Western Library:

THE CHISELLER

Tex Larrigan

Soon the paddle steamer would be on its long journey down the Missouri River to St Louis. Now, all Saul Rhymer had to do was to play the last master stroke of the evening. He looked at the mounting pile of gold and dollar bills and again at the cards in his hand. Then, looking around the table, he produced the deed to the goldmine in Montana. 'Let's play poker!' But little did he know how that journey back to St Louis would change his life so drastically.

THE ARIZONA KID

Andrew McBride

When former hired gun Calvin Taylor took the job of sheriff of Oxford County, New Mexico, it was for one reason only — to catch, or kill, the notorious Arizona Kid, and pick up the fifteen hundred dollars reward the governor had secretly offered. Taylor found himself on the trail of the infamous gang known as the Regulators, hunting down a man who'd once been his friend. The pursuit became, in every sense, a journey of death.

BULLETS IN
BUZZARDS CREEK

Bret Rey

The discovery of a dead saloon girl is only the beginning of Sheriff Jeff Gilpin's problems. Fortunately, his old friend 'Doc' Holliday arrives in Buzzards Creek just as Gilpin is faced by an outlaw gang. In a dramatic shoot-out the sheriff kills their leader and Holliday's reputation scares the hell out of the others. But it isn't long before the outlaws return, when they know Holliday is not around, and Gilpin is alone against six men . . .

THE YANKEE HANGMAN

Cole Rickard

Dan Tate was given a virtually impossible task: to save the murderer Jack Williams from the condemned cell. Williams, scum that he was, held a secret that was dear to the Confederate cause. But if saving Williams would test all Dan's ingenuity, then his further mission called for immense courage and daring. His life was truly on the line and if he didn't succeed, Horace Honeywell, the Yankee Hangman would have the last word!

MISSOURI PALACE

S. J. Rodgers

When ex-lawman Jim Williams accepts the post of security officer on the *Missouri Palace* riverboat, he finds himself embroiled in a power struggle between Captain J. D. Harris and Jake Farrell, the murderous boss of Willow Flats, who will stop at nothing to add the giant sidepaddler to his fleet. Williams knows that with no one to back him up in a straight fight with Farrell's hired killers, he must hit them first and hit them hard to get out alive.